Are You Up to Speed with the NBA HIGH-FLYERS?

Who is
(a) ... the Georgetown All-American who led the Hoyas to one national championship and into the NCAA title game in three of his four seasons?

(b) ... the "Admiral," who won the 1993–94 NBA scoring title with an incredible 71-point performance in the final game of the year?

(c) ... the Nigerian All-American who made it to the NCAA finals twice during his three seasons?

(d) ... the lefty sharpshooter who shot to the top of the league?

Read all about them as you catch up on the inside scoop on the hottest players around ...

NBA High-Flyers

Answers: (a) Patrick Ewing (b) David Robinson (c) Hakeem Olajuwon (d) Chris Mullin

Books by Bill Gutman

Sports Illustrated: BASEBALL'S RECORD BREAKERS
Sports Illustrated: GREAT MOMENTS IN BASEBALL
Sports Illustrated: GREAT MOMENTS IN PRO FOOTBALL
Sports Illustrated: PRO FOOTBALL'S RECORD BREAKERS
Sports Illustrated: STRANGE AND AMAZING BASEBALL STORIES
Sports Illustrated: STRANGE AND AMAZING FOOTBALL STORIES
BASEBALL SUPER TEAMS
BASEBALL'S HOT NEW STARS
BO JACKSON: A BIOGRAPHY
FOOTBALL SUPER TEAMS
GREAT QUARTERBACKS OF THE N.F.L.
GREAT SPORTS UPSETS
GREAT SPORTS UPSETS 2
MICHAEL JORDAN: A BIOGRAPHY
NBA HIGH-FLYERS
PRO SPORTS CHAMPIONS
SHAQUILLE O'NEAL: A BIOGRAPHY
STRANGE AND AMAZING WRESTLING STORIES

Available from ARCHWAY Paperbacks

NBA
HIGH-FLYERS

BILL
GUTMAN

AN ARCHWAY PAPERBACK
Published by POCKET BOOKS
New York   London   Toronto   Sydney   Tokyo   Singapore

AN ARCHWAY PAPERBACK *Original*

An Archway Paperback published by
POCKET BOOKS, a division of Simon & Schuster Inc.
1230 Avenue of the Americas, New York, NY 10020

Copyright © 1995 by Bill Gutman

ISBN: 0-671-88739-4

First Archway Paperback printing January 1995

10 9 8 7 6 5 4 3 2 1

AN ARCHWAY PAPERBACK and colophon are
registered trademarks of Simon & Schuster Inc.

Cover photos by Focus on Sports

Printed in the U.S.A.

IL 5+

For Cathy

Contents

INTRODUCTION

IN THE DECADE OF THE 1980s THE NATIONAL BASKET-
ball Association prospered as never before. Not only
was the caliber of basketball outstanding but the
league also made an effort to market its product to
the public on a grand scale.

During the 1970s the league had suffered from a
financial and marketing malaise. With the number of
black players on the increase, many felt that white
fans would stay away from arenas. Others felt there
were too many lazy players who didn't give their all
until the playoffs. The regular season had become little more than a walk-through. And to make matters
worse, television ratings were down.

Then in 1979–80 two players came along who
helped change the game. They were Earvin "Magic"
Johnson out of Michigan State University and Larry
Bird of Indiana State. Johnson joined the L.A. Lakers
while Bird became part of the great Boston Celtic
tradition. Both were magnificent players who gave 100

percent every night. Each played a complete team game with little regard for individual statistics and glory. They led their respective teams to the top and started a rivalry that would last for a decade.

Because of Johnson and Bird, the NBA began coming back. Then in 1984–85 another magnificent rookie came along. He was Michael Jordan of North Carolina University, who joined the Chicago Bulls and quickly established himself as the most scintillating individual talent the league had ever seen.

Add to those three many other great players and outstanding teams, plus the marketing genius of Commissioner David Stern and the NBA was on its way. Basketball was soon number one among a whole new young generation of fans, surpassing both football and baseball in popularity.

Then in the early 1990s the league had to deal with the loss of its big three. Bird retired because of a bad back; Johnson had to quit when he learned he had HIV. And Michael Jordan retired suddenly at the top of his game after leading the Chicago Bulls to three straight NBA titles. The tragic murder of his father during the off-season might have prompted his decision. Air Jordan decided to try his hand at a new challenge—baseball.

How would the league cope without its greatest stars? That was a question asked by many, and the answer came quickly. Barkley, Ewing, Mullin, Olajuwon, Robinson, Pippen, O'Neal, Johnson, and Mourning are just some of the outstanding players who have helped keep the NBA on top. Charles Barkley, Patrick Ewing, Chris Mullin, and Hakeem Olajuwon, already veterans, still entertain fans and lead their teams night after night. David Robinson and Scottie Pippen are at the peak of their careers, while Shaquille O'Neal, Larry Johnson, and Alonzo Mourning are three of the top players from the new generation, destined to lead the NBA into the twenty-first century.

Meet the NBA's greatest stars: *NBA High-Flyers* will look at the exciting careers of these nine greats, showing how these men became part of basketball's elite. These are the players who continue to make the NBA the biggest show in town.

HAKEEM OLAJUWON

As OF 1994, HAKEEM OLAJUWON WAS *THE* MAN IN the National Basketball Association. The star center of the Houston Rockets was riding a hot streak that saw him lead his team to the NBA title, win the Defensive Player of the Year Award, win the coveted Most Valuable Player prize, and also take MVP laurels for the playoffs.

The Nigerian-born Olajuwon is almost unanimously being called the best player in the league. No easy accomplishment, especially when you consider that Hakeem never even touched a basketball until he was in his teens.

Hakeem Abdul Olajuwon was born on January 21, 1963, in Lagos, a large city of nearly six million people in Nigeria, a country in Africa.

There was a great deal of poverty and unemployment in Lagos, but Hakeem's parents, Salaam and Abike, ran a cement business. They weren't rich, but they weren't poor, either. Hakeem grew up with four brothers and a sister. So it was a large family living in a one-story three-bedroom house behind a small fenced-in courtyard. Hakeem's parents encouraged all their children to get an education so they could live better lives.

As a youngster, Hakeem was shy and went out of his way to avoid fights. But he grew quickly and was always the tallest boy in his age group. The two sports he played were soccer and handball.

His father, Salaam Olajuwon, was 6'3" tall, but Hakeem passed him quickly. When one of the few basketball coaches in Lagos spotted him at age 15 he was nearly 6'9" and 170 pounds. The coach's name was Ganiyu Otenigbade, and he talked the youngster into trying the new game. That was in 1978.

A year later Hakeem was playing with the Lagos State juniors in a club league. They played on an asphalt court with tilted backboards.

By 1980 Hakeem was a member of the Nigerian national team and played in the All-African Games, held in Morocco. He played very well in the competition, and the Nigerian team got the bronze medal for third place. Hakeem was also attending Moslem Teachers College in Lagos—the equivalent of a high school in the United States. The school's basketball team wasn't very good, so Hakeem's only real experience was with the national team.

Going to college in the United States was an idea that appealed to Hakeem's whole family. Chris Pond, who was working with the U.S. State Department and doing some coaching, recommended that Hakeem visit the University of Houston. Pond was an old friend of Houston coach Guy Lewis and told him about the youngster who was close to seven feet tall.

Hakeem planned to visit seven schools, but chose Houston as soon as he saw the campus. In October of 1980, Hakeem arrived on the UH campus. As soon as Coach Lewis saw the big kid from Lagos he knew two things. One was that Hakeem had a world of natural ability and tremendous potential. The other was that he had never been taught the fundamentals of basketball.

Communication for Hakeem wasn't a problem. He spoke English, French, and four Nigerian dialects. His English was precise and spoken with a British accent. But because his basketball skills were so rough, Coach Lewis decided to redshirt him. That meant he wouldn't play in 1980–81, but would still have four years of eligibility after that.

So Hakeem began to work on his game. Two years earlier he hadn't even known how to dunk the ball or make a simple layup.

"I had no idea how to use the glass," Hakeem admitted. "I used to just try to push it in. I remember one game in Nigeria when I missed a layup and got so mad I didn't go back on defense. After we lost, I wanted to give up, just not play the game anymore."

When the 1981–82 season came around, Hakeem was ready to join the Cougar varsity, a team that included stars Clyde Drexler, Rob Williams, and Larry Micheaux.

"When I came to Houston, I didn't know what I could do," Hakeem said. "I was just happy to be on the team. I had watched the first year, but thought, 'I can do this.' "

The Cougars had a good team that year, and Coach Lewis wanted to work his big guy into the lineup as often as possible. But Hakeem found out something else about this sport, which was still so new for him: he wasn't in game shape.

Early in the season he began getting back spasms. He wasn't doing enough stretching exercises. A number of times he would go up for a dunk and come down holding his back. Or, if he was on the court for a very fast-paced five-minute stretch, he would become exhausted. He also would accumulate fouls too quickly and have to sit down.

"I kept him out of games," said Coach Lewis. "And I wouldn't let him practice till he could run. That first year he never did get to where he could play a full game. There were times when he hurt us because you can't play up-tempo when four guys are running and the other is dyin'. I don't care how you slice it. That first year he flat out didn't know how to play."

Lewis did say that Hakeem was already becoming a fine shot blocker. But he still had a long way to go. One thing that already burned within Hakeem was the desire to succeed, the will to win. Not playing made him angry.

Though the team was unranked at the end of the regular season, having lost seven games, they surprised everyone by making it to the Final Four of the NCAA tournament. There they lost to the eventual champ, North Carolina, 68–63, to finish the year at 25-8. But even in the final game, Hakeem played very little.

"I didn't start, and they're coming down the lane shooting layups," Hakeem said. "I was so mad I was burning up."

Hakeem averaged 8.3 points and 6.2 rebounds in 1981–82. He blocked 72 shots and had a high game of 20 points against LSU and 8 blocks against TCU. Though he was angry because he didn't play more,

Hakeem used his anger constructively. He was determined to become an outstanding player. And considering it was his first real basketball season ever, he did quite well.

During the off-season, and especially during the summer, Hakeem worked out constantly. He often went to the Fonde Recreation Center in Houston where a number of NBA stars, past and present, played. One regular was Moses Malone, then considered one of the best centers in the NBA.

"I played against a lot of pro players without knowing who they were," Hakeem said. "People would have to tell me, 'He's a pro,' or 'He used to be a pro.' But because of the summer, I came back to Houston knowing I could play."

With a returning nucleus of Drexler, Michaeax, Michael Young, and Alvin Franklin, Hakeem provided the final piece to the puzzle. It was apparent from the outset that he was a different ballplayer. He hadn't just improved; he had become a star and a major force. The Cougars began rolling over opponents with such force and certainty that the club became known as Phi Slamma Jamma, a play on the Greek letters used in naming college fraternities. The "Slamma Jamma" came from the fact that Hakeem, Drexler, and their teammates loved dunking the basketball and seemed to slam and jam it home more often than any other team in the country. And as the team began running over opponents, Hakeem began putting together some real big games.

When the regular season ended, the Cougars had a 27-2 record and were the number one ranked team in the nation. They were given the top seed in the Midwest Regional and were the favorites to win the

At the University of Houston, Hakeem was the leader of the team nicknamed Phi Slamma Jamma. And the big guy slammed the ball home more than anyone else. *(Photo courtesy University of Houston)*

NCAA tournament. And though Hakeem had enjoyed an outstanding regular season, it was his work in the NCAAs that really gave everyone a glimpse of what was to come.

First Maryland fell easily, then Memphis State and Villanova in the regional final as the Cougars advanced to the Final Four at Albuquerque. Hakeem played so well that he was named the Most Outstanding Player at the Midwest Regional.

In the semifinals the Cougars went up against a fine Louisville team and came out on top, 94–81. Hakeem had been amazing. He finished with 21 points, 22 big rebounds, and 8 blocked shots. In the second half alone he had 12 points, 15 rebounds, and 4 blocks.

"It's almost impossible to believe that five years ago this kid had never played basketball," one writer covering the game said. "He looks so strong and dominant that there probably isn't an NBA team that wouldn't take him right now."

The Cougars had one more game to play, against the Cinderella team of the tourney, North Carolina State. The Wolfpack had gotten a berth in the tournament with only a 20-10 record. But then they began winning. Jim Valvano's team was patient and growing in confidence. The Cougars were overwhelming favorites, but the Wolfpack didn't panic. They tried to slow their pace, take good shots, and prevent Phi Slamma Jamma from fast breaking.

The strategy worked, especially when Coach Lewis ordered his team to slow the action with some nine minutes still remaining and Houston with a small lead. With two minutes left, a Wolfpack hoop tied the game at 52. Still, Lewis continued the stall. With a minute left, Alvin Franklin was fouled. But he missed the front end of a one-and-one, giving the ball to State. Now Valvano's club played for a last shot. With the seconds ticking down, Derrick Whittenburg tried a long jumper. The ball was short. But suddenly State's Lorenzo Charles rose up to catch the air ball and slam it home just before the buzzer.

State had won, 54–52, in a major upset. Some pointed their fingers at Hakeem for not boxing Charles out. But he had started out to challenge the shot, then turned to hold his position for a rebound. Charles had sneaked inside him and gotten the hoop.

Up to that point, Hakeem had dominated the game, scoring 20 points, grabbing 18 rebounds, and blocking an amazing 11 shots. He was named Most Valuable Player for the Final Four, even though his team had lost. In fact, for five tournament games he had averaged 18.8 points, 13 rebounds, and 6.4 blocks. He had also shot 65.6 percent from the floor. For the season he had scored at a 13.9 clip, grabbed 11.4 rebounds, and blocked 175 shots for an average of 5.1, best in the nation.

"When I think about that game I try not to think about the last minute," Hakeem would say. "I feel too bad just mentioning it. I know I don't want to be in that position again or feel like that again. It was heartbreaking."

Strangely enough, Hakeem didn't make a whole lot of All-American teams. He was still grouped below Ralph Sampson and Patrick Ewing, who were the consensus All-American centers. But Hakeem figured his time was coming, and he went right back to work in the off-season, once again working out with Moses Malone and other pros.

"This summer was different," he would say. "The

last two years Moses was just pushing me around using his body. This summer I fought back. I decided I can't just be looking up to him all the time."

Hakeem also worked with weights, and when he returned for the 1983–84 season he was close to seven feet tall and weighed nearly 250 pounds. No wonder he'd decided to push back. The team would be slightly different this year: Micheaux was gone, and Drexler had decided to turn pro a year early. Hakeem thought about going, too, but decided he would be worth more money if he played another year.

Hakeem came back an even better player than the year before. It didn't take long for the numbers to start coming. On December 3 he blocked an incredible 16 shots in a game against Biscayne. A few weeks later he scored a career high 35 points against UC Santa Barbara. In January he had 25 rebounds against Texas Tech. In the Santa Barbara game he had made 15 of 17 shots from the floor. He was 14 of 16 against Wake Forest and was perfect against Baylor and Arkansas, hitting all 17 shots he took in both games.

He could do a lot more than just jam now. He could shoot the jumper and the hook, and he was developing very quick spin moves around the basket. His first step was incredibly quick for a man of his size. He began drawing raves wherever he played.

It was that way all year. Hakeem had become a superstar center. At the end of the regular season the Cougars had a 21-7 record and were ranked fifth nationally. In the NCAA tournament Houston again began playing well. They won the Midwest Regional and another trip to the Final Four, their third in three years.

In the semifinals the Virginia Cavaliers played a

slow-down game and almost won it. But Houston prevailed, 49–47, to set up a title game showdown with Georgetown and its seven-foot center, Patrick Ewing.

The game was billed as a battle between the two top centers in the country, but it turned into something else. Hakeem was called for a third foul just before the half, then committed his fourth just 23 seconds into the second half. So he had to sit out for a significant amount of time.

In the end Georgetown's swarming defense probably made the difference. The Hoyas won the national crown, 84–75. Hakeem wound up with 15 points and 9 rebounds, while Ewing had just 10 points and nine boards. It was another disappointment for Hakeem and the rest of the Cougars.

Hakeem finished the year with a 16.8 scoring average in 37 games. His 500 total rebounds led the nation and gave him a 13.5 average. He also led the nation with 207 blocked shots, an average of 5.6 a game. In addition, he shot an amazing 67.5 percent from the field. He was a consensus All-American, though surprisingly he didn't win any of the major Player of the Year prizes.

He had now been at Houston for four years. Because he was redshirted as a freshman he had another year of eligibility. But he knew it was time to move on: he was ready for the NBA. He informed everyone that he was entering the 1984 draft.

The two teams vying for the first pick in the draft were the Houston Rockets and the Portland Trail Blazers. The choice was made by a coin flip, the winner getting the top pick. The Rockets won the toss. And that created a strange situation.

Houston had also won the toss the year before, and

had immediately picked 7'4" center Ralph Sampson of Virginia. That had come after a 14-68 season in 1982–83. With Sampson averaging 21 points, 11.1 rebounds, and 2.4 blocks, the team seemingly had found an outstanding center. But their record improved to only 29-53. Now the question was, would they take another center?

It didn't take long for the Rockets to make a decision. They picked Hakeem, making him the top choice of the entire league. Rockets fans began wondering just how Coach Bill Fitch would play Sampson and Olajuwon. Maybe they wanted to see which big man would develop into the better player, then trade the other one.

Unlike the inexperienced freshman who had come to Houston in 1980, Hakeem joined the Rockets with confidence, knowing that he could compete in the NBA. After signing a six-year contract worth some $6.3 million, he then went out and proved it. He was now being called by a new nickname, Hakeem the Dream. And from the start, he seemed able to coexist with the 7'4" Sampson.

During the preseason it became apparent that Hakeem was more of a power player than the lanky Sampson. If the two big men were going to be on the court at the same time, one of them would have to move to power forward. It was generally Hakeem who set up in the low post closer to the basket. Sampson preferred to operate from a little farther out.

The opening game of the 1984–85 season saw the Rockets topple the Dallas Mavericks, 121–111. Hakeem started slowly, then came on strong, scoring 22 of his 24 points in the second half. He also had 9 rebounds. Sampson also played well, finishing with 19 points and 13 rebounds.

"I guess the court was big enough for both of them," quipped Coach Fitch.

It wasn't long before the two were dubbed "the Twin Towers," and they were instrumental in the Rockets becoming winners.

By the end of the season the Rockets were a 48-34 team, finishing second in the Midwest Division and showing a 19-game improvement from the season before. Hakeem finished his rookie year by averaging 20.6 points and 11.9 rebounds. He blocked 220 shots. Sampson led the team in scoring with a 22.1 point average, grabbed 10.4 rebounds, and blocked 168 shots. It might have been the most successful coupling of two big men in NBA history.

Unfortunately, the Rockets were eliminated by the Utah Jazz in the first round of the playoffs, 3–2. Still, it had been a great year. Hakeem finished second to Michael Jordan in the Rookie of the Year voting.

In 1985–86, the Twin Towers concept once again seemed to work very well. But there were also a few telltale signs that Hakeem Olajuwon was beginning to assert himself as *the* big man on the Rockets. Houston came on to win the Midwest Division with a 51-31 mark.

Despite missing 14 games with a sore knee, Hakeem led the team in scoring with a 23.5 mark. He averaged 11.5 rebounds and blocked 231 shots, a 3.4 average. Sampson's scoring average was down to 18.9 points in 79 games. He averaged 11.9 rebounds and blocked 129 shots, or 1.6 a game. But no one was thinking about numbers as the Rockets made a run at the NBA title.

In the first round the Rockets swept the Sacramento

Kings in three games. Then they whipped Denver in six. Next came the Western Conference finals, and the Rockets humbled Magic Johnson, Kareem Abdul-Jabbar, and the L.A. Lakers in just five games. Hakeem was the leading scorer in four of them, posting games of 28, 40, 35 and 30 points.

Now the club was in the finals against Larry Bird and the Boston Celtics. The Celts were just a little too tough. Houston fought hard, but was beaten in six games. Hakeem had highs of 33 and 32 against Boston. In 20 playoff games he had averaged 26.9 points and 11.8 boards.

The following year the Rockets took a backward step. Sampson played in just 43 games. The injuries that would ultimately cut his effectiveness and shorten his career had begun. Hakeem had another outstanding year, but the Rockets were just 42-40, and they were bumped from the playoffs in the second round. But the big guy went out with a bang. In a double-overtime loss to Seattle that eliminated the Rockets, Hakeem put in a career high 49 points.

Then in 1987–88, the shape of the team changed. In December, Ralph Sampson was traded to Golden State for center Joe Barry Carroll and guard Sleepy Floyd. Hakeem was now the one and only man in the middle. Yet while the club continued to post winning records for the next couple of years, they had a hard time getting past the first round of the playoffs.

In 1988–89 Hakeem averaged a career best 24.8 points; he was tenth best in the league and the top scoring center. He led the league in rebounding with a 13.5 mark, was fourth in blocks (3.44 per game) and, amazingly, sixth in steals with 2.60 thefts per game. He was the only center in the top ten in steals. By this time, Hakeem was a first team All-NBA star, named for the third straight season. He had also been selected to the Western Conference All-Star team for five straight years.

But he wasn't happy with the makeup of the team and began speaking out. He even criticized some teammates for selfish play and lack of desire.

"All I was saying is you don't build with these guys," he said. It's okay to have one or two guys like that, but not a whole team of them."

The team was 41-41 in 1989–90, with Hakeem leading the league in rebounding and blocks. The next year saw more of the same. On January 3, 1991, the Rockets were 16-13 and playing the Chicago Bulls. During a scramble under the hoop, Bulls center Bill Cartwright whirled around, elbow first, and inadvertently caught Hakeem square in the face. The blow fractured Olajuwon's right orbit, the bone that houses the eye. Hakeem needed surgery and was out indefinitely.

Without the big guy it was thought the Rockets would crumble. Indeed they did lose seven of the first ten games he missed. But with 6'8" veteran Larry Smith filling in and rebounding like a demon, the ball club began to win. Suddenly they were on a 12-of-15 tear.

In Hakeem's absence, power forward Otis Thorpe and guards Sleepy Floyd, Vernon Maxwell, and Kenny Smith all raised the level of their games. There was more passing to the open man, more action, a faster-paced team game. Even the fans got into it more. Without Hakeem, the Rockets had evolved into winners.

It seemed that the other players had come to depend on him too much. While he was out, they rediscovered themselves, and team basketball. Sleepy Floyd spoke for the rest of the team when he said, "He [Hakeem] comes back and takes us to the next level."

Hakeem returned on February 28. He, too, had marveled at what he saw. "Guys diving for the ball, hungry guys," he said. "It was like, 'Look at me.' They had a chance to show what they could do."

It was easy for Hakeem to fit in with his teammates, and it didn't go back to the way it was. The Rockets continued to play their new brand of ball, and Hakeem loved it.

"Ever since I came into this league I've been double-teamed," he said. "But now that the offense is spread out, the game is suddenly easy. It's like in college. It's fun. When the game is over now, I'm not even tired. I could play another game."

The Rockets finished the season with a surprising 51-30 record, third in the Midwest. But again they were foiled in the playoffs. Still, the kind of team play they had discovered might have marked the beginning of a new era. In 1991–92, after another year of internal strife, the club slipped to 42-40 and missed the playoffs. Some 52 games into the season Rudy Tomjanovich, a former Rocket, took over as coach. Everyone looked to 1992–93 for a fresh start.

The team added a rookie forward named Robert Horry and some additional role players. Now the nucleus was Hakeem, Thorpe, Horry, Smith, and Maxwell. And with Hakeem having a tremendous year, the team began to win. Just after midseason it was announced that Hakeem had signed a four-year contract extension worth some $26–30 million.

He was playing so well that he was being talked about as a possible Most Valuable Player. Veteran center-forward Wayman Tisdale of Sacramento spoke for many when he said no one was better than Olajuwon: "You can compare these great centers all you want and not figure out who's best. All I know is, there's no one *better* than Hakeem. He protects the basket like it's his own little cubbyhole. It amazes me that people continue to take it to the basket against him."

Offensively Hakeem's speed was even more apparent. He had more moves underneath than Ewing, David Robinson, and rookie Shaquille O'Neal, the other top centers of the mid-1990s.

"I see my game as something creative, maybe something new," the Dream said. "More moves, more fakes, more of the unexpected. I get great joy from losing my man completely."

The Rockets finished the 1992–93 season as Midwest Division winners with a 55-27 record. Hakeem was fourth in scoring at 26.1, fourth in rebounds, and first in blocked shots. The only disappointment was being eliminated in the Conference semifinals by Seattle, 4–3. So coming into the 1993–94 season, the Rockets felt they had some unfinished business.

They didn't waste any time. Incredibly, the team opened the season with 15 straight wins, surprising everyone. The same nucleus was still there. Rookie guard Sam Cassell had taken Floyd's place, while Carl Herrera provided size off the bench. Thorpe and Horry were a pair of 6'10" forwards who emphasized defense. And in the middle, Hakeem was playing better than ever.

He would be 31 years old before the season

ended, but it was apparent he was at the top of his game. In a year when all the top centers—Ewing, Robinson, O'Neal, Mutombo, Mourning—seemed to be dominating the league, Hakeem was the number one guy. And by the time the regular season ended, Hakeem was being talked about as a surefire MVP.

The Rockets finished as Midwest champs once again, this time with a franchise record 58-24 mark, second best to Seattle in the entire league. Hakeem wrapped up his greatest regular season third in scoring with a 27.3 average, fourth in rebounding with 11.9 per game, and second in blocks at 3.71 per contest. Those were the numbers. It was all the little things he did—passing, intimidation, leadership—that made him special.

Then it was time for the playoffs. The Rockets started by whipping the Portland Trail Blazers in four. Next, they had to face Charles Barkley and the talented Phoenix Suns. The Suns won the first two games at Houston. But Houston rebounded to take two at Phoenix and then game five back home for a 3–2 lead.

Phoenix wouldn't quit, and it came down to a seventh game. Houston won it, 104–94, as Hakeem rose to the occasion with 37 points and 17 rebounds. Now it was on to the conference finals against the Utah Jazz. During the playoffs it was announced that Hakeem had been chosen Defensive Player of the Year for the second straight time and had made the All-Defensive team for the fifth time in his career. A short time later he was named the NBA's Most Valuable Player. At last.

With the Rockets hitting their stride, Utah fell in five games. Now it was on to the finals. Hakeem and his teammates would be meeting the physical New York Knicks and their center, Patrick Ewing, a great jump shooter and an outstanding scorer, as well as a fine shot blocker. But the consensus was that Hakeem had the better all-around game.

It turned into a tight-knit, physical defensive series, the kind of basketball that would seem to have favored the Knicks. The teams split the first two games at Houston, the Rockets winning, 85–78, then the Knicks coming out on top, 91–83. Hakeem did not have a strong fourth quarter in either game, and some felt he was tired from the long season.

The Rockets put away game three in New York in the final seconds when a double-teamed Hakeem threw an outlet pass to rookie Cassell, who promptly drilled a three-pointer. The final was 93–89. Game four went to the Knicks, 91–82, and in game five at Madison Square Garden, the Knicks won it with an 11–1 run in the final three minutes. Their 91–84 victory gave them a 3–2 lead, and Houston was on the brink of elimination.

Game six was like all the rest. It came down to this: the Rockets had an 86–84 lead with 5.5 seconds left. The ball went to John Starks, who had a hot hand. Just before the buzzer, Starks launched a three-pointer. If it went in, the Knicks would be champs. But Hakeem came out, leaped high in the air, and got a piece of the ball as Starks released it. It fell short, and the Rockets had tied the series.

Now there was one game left for the title. For Hakeem, this meant everything, even more than the MVP. "A championship is team glory," he said, "where the MVP is an individual honor. You always have to take the team first."

Hakeem's fadeaway jump shot is almost impossible to stop. Here he gets it off against one of his arch rivals, Patrick Ewing of the Knicks. *(John Biever photo)*

The final game was like all the others, physical and close. Neither team could break it open. Only the Knicks weren't shooting well. Guard John Starks, who had been a major factor in several Knicks wins, was 0-11 from three-point range and 2-18 for the game. The Houston guards, criticized for much of the series, played well. And then there was Hakeem.

Once again Olajuwon outplayed Patrick Ewing, and when it ended, the Rockets had a 90–84 victory. They were champions, riding home on a 25-point, 10-rebound, 7-assist performance by their star center. Guard Kenny Smith said it all: "With one game for the championship, you have to think that the best player on your team is going to carry you to the title. I'm sure the Knicks felt like Ewing would do that for them. But we *knew* Hakeem would do it for us."

To no one's surprise, Hakeem was the MVP of the playoffs. For the seven games against the Knicks he had averaged 26.9 points, grabbed 93 rebounds, and blocked 3.9 shots a game. And he held Ewing to 58 for 160 shooting, a 36.2 percent mark. He had done it all.

The season had been Hakeem's crowning glory. The league's Most Valuable Player, Defensive Player of the Year, the playoff MVP, the world champion—it had been a long time coming.

"In the locker room I just sat back and reflected," Hakeem said. "I saw everybody celebrating. That was something you picture in your mind before. But I actually enjoyed that moment of peace, just watching everyone celebrating."

It was surely something he had earned. When you remember that Hakeem never touched a basketball until he was 15, then became a consensus All-American some six years later, well, it's an amazing story, a story that would not have been complete without an NBA championship.

CHARLES BARKLEY

SOME REGARD HIM AS THE BAD BOY OF THE NBA, A say-anything-do-anything character who can be charming one minute, nasty the next. Others call him Sir Charles and consider him a supremely talented player who gives 100 percent night in and night out. His only fault might be that he's too honest, too candid, and often speaks out when discretion might be called for.

"I'm not a role model," Charles Barkley has insisted over the years, debunking the notion that athletes should be role models for youngsters, and in recent years many other athletes as well as psychologists and educators have come to agree with him. Charles even made a television commercial to that effect.

Charles Barkley made the commercial because that's what he believes—that parents, not athletes, should be the principal role models for their children. Straight talk in stating his beliefs is part of being Charles Barkley. He may be one of the straightest shooters among professional athletes. If he has an opinion, he'll voice it. He admits to being a ferocious competitor in a rough game. He's also an emotional player who has done things in the heat of battle that he's later regretted. Yet those who know him well say he's not only a very honest man but a decent one as well.

None of this, however, should distract from Charles Barkley's ability on the basketball court. He is simply an incredible player. Though most press guides list him as 6'6", many have said that he is no taller than 6'4½". But that inch-and-a-half notwithstanding, Charles Barkley does some amazing things on the basketball court.

He was a center at Auburn University, but he can play nearly every position on the court. He is always up among the rebound leaders in the NBA and led the league in that category in 1986–87. He can score from the inside against much taller defenders, can shoot the three, can create on offense and can slam-dunk with anyone. Yet there was a time—when he was a 5'10" high school junior, and again when he was a 305-pound college center—when most people thought Charles Barkley would never fit into the NBA.

Charles grew up in Leeds, Alabama, where he was born on February 20, 1963. In his early years, he wasn't a great athlete, and there were no signs that he would grow up to be a superstar. He wasn't especially tall, and he was always on the heavy side, with an appetite that wouldn't quit.

He played all sports as a youngster, with basketball slowly emerging as his best sport. But even when he entered Leeds High School there was no indication that he would be something special. When he started his junior year he was still 5'10", 220 pounds, and while fundamentally sound, he didn't have the interest of the colleges.

But that year Leeds began to win, and Charles began to grow. That was when things started changing. Leeds was 26-3 in Charles's junior season and made it to the 3A state tournament. Then came his senior year, 1980–81. Now Charles was well over six feet and still growing. Though he was a fine offensive player, it was his defense and rebounding that began attracting attention.

Already around the 240-pound mark, Charles would just move other players out of the way when he went for the ball. And despite his weight, he was an outstanding leaper who was very quick off the floor. He scored 33 points in one game and grabbed an amazing 30 rebounds in another.

When the season ended, Charles had an average of 19.1 points a game while grabbing 17.9 rebounds and blocking 5 shots per contest. He also hit 59.7 percent of his field goal tries and led the team to a 25-7 record. He was now considered one of the top five prep prospects in Alabama.

It's not surprising that schools from his home state of Alabama were the ones who pursued him the most vigorously. Charles finally decided to stay close to home and attend Auburn University. He entered Auburn in the fall of 1981. At first glance the coaches and other players weren't sure what they were getting.

Here was a guy not quite 6'6" and more than 260 pounds who looked as wide as he was tall. Yet he was supposed to be a center. Centers, as a rule, were 6'9" and taller. Usually the taller the better. What use could an 18-year-old overweight kid from Leeds possibly be?

On the court, Charles had some bad habits. He played hard only when he felt like it, whether at practice or in a game. But it didn't take Coach Sonny Smith and his staff long to see the tremendous potential in Charles's rather round and large body.

For one thing, he was deceptively fast for a man his size. He was a good jumper, but so were a lot of other guys. Charles, however, was also a very quick jumper. He could get off the floor before his opponents and go up a second time while they were just thinking about it. He was also a good shooter and fine defender. His quickness enabled him to block the shots of taller opponents.

By the sixth game of the 1981–82 season Charles had become a starter. He was still somewhat inconsistent. The coaches and his teammates could never be sure which Charles Barkley would show up, the one who was an unstoppable force or the one who just went through the motions.

"We were lucky if he played hard in practice that first year," said assistant coach Mack McCarthy. "It wasn't important to him. He was a good player, and if he proved it once a week, that was okay."

But it wasn't long before Charles's natural talent showed through. For instance, when Auburn rolled into Adolph Rupp Arena in Lexington to play mighty Kentucky, an average freshman might have been intimidated. Before the game, the fans really began giving him the business, mostly because of his size. Unfazed by it all, Charles began blowing kisses to them in return. Then he took the court against Kentucky's 6'11" center, Mel Turpin. Though Kentucky would eventually win the game, 81–73, it was the freshman Barkley who garnered most of the attention.

All Charles did that night was score 25 points and grab 17 rebounds while eating the bigger Turpin alive.

"He really shocked me," Turpin said. "I thought, 'Is this the right guy?'"

That wasn't Charles's only big game. He had 21 points and 11 rebounds against Tennessee and then 19 points and 16 rebounds against LSU, to name two others. By the 12th game he had set a school record for blocked shots and would wind up with 51. Seven of them came against LSU. In 28 games he was in double-figures scoring seventeen times and rebounding fifteen times.

When the season ended, Charles was second team all-Southeastern Conference and a third team freshman All-American. He was only the second freshman ever to lead the SEC in rebounding. For the year he averaged 12.7 points a game and 9.8 rebounds. He also shot an outstanding 59.5 percent from the floor. Yet he averaged just nine shots a game.

Charles had been gaining weight throughout the season. After it ended, he was one of four SEC players chosen to represent the South in the National Sports Festival in Indianapolis. His weight at festival time was said to be just over 300 pounds. Yet he was still good enough to score 20 points and grab 11 rebounds as the South won, 125–114.

About a month before practice started for his sophomore season he began running three miles a day and watching his diet. He got his weight down to about 265, but he still didn't always give 100 percent effort.

It was also a year in which he began acquiring his many nicknames. At one time or another, Charles was referred to as Fat Boy, Bread Truck, Food World, the Crisco Kid, the Love Boat, the Leaning Tower of Pizza, the Goodtime Blimp, and the Round Mound of Rebound. It was the last one—the Round Mound of Rebound—that would last the longest.

As a sophomore Charles had more good days than bad, but his numbers were similar to those of his freshman season. He averaged 14.4 points a game and grabbed 266 rebounds in 28 games. Once again he was the SEC rebounding leader and, in the eyes of many, one of the conference's better players.

The problem was that Auburn wasn't a traditional basketball powerhouse. Finally in 1983–84, the team became more than respectable. They had a scoring star to support Charles—forward Chuck Person would average nearly 20 points a game. The team also had improved guard play and looked for a big season, maybe even an SEC title.

As for Charles, he returned a different person. Suddenly he had a positive attitude that was even reflected in his classroom performance: he maintained a B average. At practice he went all out every day. It was as if he was now ready to meet any and all challenges.

Charles himself acknowledged his change in attitude. "I've gotten more mature," he said. "In the past few years I would have rebelled against him [Coach Smith]. This year I'm learning to work with him. It just took me two years to learn he was right."

A back injury in the preseason put him on the shelf for a while. He missed three early games and played in just parts of several others. But once he was at full strength, he started opening people's eyes wherever he went, and the Tigers began winning.

In a 65–60 victory over Florida, he scored 28 points, though his season average was at 13.7. Then on January 13 the Tigers hosted Kentucky, the Wildcats coming in as the number-one–ranked team in the country. Enter Charles Barkley. The Round Mound hit on seven of eleven shots from the field, scored 21 points, grabbed 10 boards, and blocked three shots as Auburn pulled off the upset in a big way, 82–63.

"Charles Barkley intimidates a lot of people," said seven-foot Kentucky forward/center Sam Bowie. "He's as strong as any player in the country. Anybody who tells you they're not intimidated by him is lying."

In a 10-game run started by the win over Kentucky, Charles averaged 19.2 points, 10.9 rebounds, and 2.6 blocked shots. In addition, he was shooting 67.3 percent from the field.

"In recent games Charles Barkley has become the type player I always thought he would be—a total player," said Coach Smith. "He is putting things together better than he ever has. His rebounding and outlet passes have made our fast break one of the better parts of our game this year."

Teammate Gerald White, a freshman point guard, was also impressed with Charles. "When Charles gets the ball on a rebound and starts up the court," White said, "everybody steps out of the way."

As the season wore on, there was talk about Charles passing up his senior year at Auburn to enter the NBA draft.

"No matter what I want to be in life, I just want to be successful at it," he said. "If I take care of my mother and grandmother, my goals in life will be complete."

He also said he would talk with his family before

making a decision. "And if I think I'm physically and mentally ready, I will go pro," he said.

A couple of tough late-season losses cost the Tigers the SEC title. They finished second to Kentucky with an 18-9 record. But considering they had never finished higher than eighth before, it was a special year. Unfortunately the team didn't win the SEC tourney and was then eliminated quickly from the NCAA tournament. So there was no fairy-tale ending.

Charles finished the year with a 15.1 scoring average, 265 rebounds in 28 games, and a 63.8 shooting percentage. He was the SEC rebounding leader for a third straight season and an All-Conference selection, but he wasn't a consensus first or second team All-American.

Shortly after the season ended, Charles ended the suspense by announcing that he would leave Auburn to head for the NBA. There was a bumper crop of collegians coming out, and the guesswork started. Houston picked first and took center Hakeem Olajuwon. Next came Portland, and they surprised everyone by taking center Sam Bowie of Kentucky.

Chicago was next. They quickly picked another junior coming out early. His name was Michael Jordan. Jordan's teammate, Sam Perkins, went to Dallas as the fourth pick. Next came the Philadelphia 76ers. The Sixers wasted no time in making Charles Barkley the fifth pick in the 1984 draft.

At the time Charles was drafted, the Sixers were coming off nine straight winning seasons. Just two years earlier, in 1982–83, the club had finished with a 65-17 regular season mark and had gone on to win the NBA championship. That club was led by the great forward Julius "Dr. J" Erving, center Moses Malone, and guard Maurice Cheeks.

The year before Charles arrived, the club was 52-30, and still one of the better teams in the NBA. With the Round Mound of Rebound joining the ball club, there was the promise of even more success.

Charles played a supporting role his rookie year. Malone was the team's star, with the aging Erving (at 35) starting to slow down but still a force on occasions. Cheeks was an outstanding point guard and floor leader. Even with these great veterans, Charles Barkley soon showed he belonged.

As he came off the bench a good part of the year, his numbers were impressive. He quickly showed in the NBA the same qualities he had shown at Auburn: the ability to score both inside and out, the toughness to guard bigger men, and the tenacity to rebound with anyone.

When the season ended, the Sixers had a 58-24 record, finishing five games behind Boston in the Atlantic Division. Charles played in all 82 games, scoring 1,148 points for a 14.0 average and grabbing 703 rebounds for an 8.6 per game norm. He also had 155 assists, 95 steals, and 80 blocked shots. In addition he shot a solid 54.5 from the field and 73.3 from the foul line.

Chicago's Michael Jordan was a runaway choice for Rookie of the Year, but Charles easily made the All-Rookie Team. He had silenced those critics who thought he might become an NBA player without a position. On the contrary, he was a player who could be comfortable at nearly every position.

In the playoffs, the Sixers made it all the way to the Eastern Conference finals, where they were beaten by archrival Boston in five games. Charles averaged

Charles was a fierce competitor from his first day in the NBA. Here, as a member of the Philadelphia 76ers, he celebrates a hoop with a pair of clenched fists. *(John Biever photo)*

14.9 points and 11.1 rebounds in 13 playoff games, elevating his numbers under playoff pressure, another mark of a great player.

It took only one more season for Charles to become a bona fide NBA star. With Erving now on the downside and Malone slowed by injury, Charles began to emerge as the Sixers go-to guy. Now playing almost thirty-seven minutes a game, he was the team's second leading scorer, behind Malone, with a 20.0 average. He also led the club in rebounds with 1,026, an average of 12.8 a game, an amazing stat for a player some said was just 6'4½" tall.

In addition, he had 312 assists, 173 steals, and 125 blocks. The team finished at 54-28, second to Boston by a big 13-game margin. In the playoffs the team lost to the Milwaukee Bucks in the Eastern Conference semifinals in seven games. Charles averaged 25 points and 15.7 rebounds in 12 playoff games, again raising his numbers from the regular season.

After it was over, he was the winner of the Shick Pivotal Player Award, given to the player who demonstrates all-around excellence. Charles certainly had the all-around stats.

When asked how a player his size could be so effective underneath, Charles was quick with a quip: "I'm like Christmas, because you know I'm coming," he said. "The main thing for me is to be the first one off the floor. Nobody in the league can jump as quick as I can, and that's important. I watch the flight of the ball carefully, whether I'm on offense or defense. I never take my eyes off it. Never. And I can usually tell where it's going."

Celtics great Larry Bird had his own explanation for Charles's effectiveness underneath. "Charles jumps from side to side, not just straight up," Bird said. "And he gets both hands on almost every ball, so he doesn't lose any."

Over the next few years the shape of the Sixers began changing. After Charles's second season the club traded Moses Malone to Washington. The 1986–87 season would prove to be the last for the great Julius Erving. And while this was happening, Charles Barkley continued to emerge as the new team leader.

In 1986–87, Barkley averaged 23.0 points a game and led the league with 994 rebounds. An injury limited him to 68 games, so his rebounding average was an impressive 14.6 a game. His field goal percentage was up to 59.4, and he had 331 assists, nearly five a game. Once again he was named the winner of the Shick Award. He was becoming an All-Pro.

Before the following season, Charles was named a Sixer co-captain along with Maurice Cheeks. He was also beginning to get a reputation as an outspoken athlete. At that time, his usual target was the Sixers.

During the previous season he had called some of his teammates "wimps and complainers." He also said he wasn't sure he wanted to be a captain, because "none of these guys can take criticism."

More and more often Charles was being described as "different" and "unique." He was like a firecracker waiting to explode; his competitiveness had become that intense. Coach Matt Guokas said, "Charles is definitely our leader, but it's not the normal type of leadership because Charles isn't your normal type of person."

Then, in the 1987–88 season, Charles Barkley emerged as one of the elite players in the NBA. He was putting together an incredible season, up near the top in a number of offensive and defensive categories. Ironically, it was the first season that the Sixers were struggling to play .500 ball. That was another reason Charles was so intense. He hated losing.

"This team is just bad," he proclaimed after a December loss to the Lakers. "Unless we play a perfect game, we can't win, and that's a bad situation to be in."

He began having words with fans who taunted him when the team was losing, and he admitted, "Sometimes the slightest thing makes me go crazy."

It was apparent, though, that Charles had raised the level of his game by several notches. He explained why: "I made up my mind last summer that if we were going to have a bad team I was not going to be the reason. I knew it was my turn to take over the team."

There were nights when he was unbelievable, as in one game against the Knicks at Madison Square Garden in New York on December 17. He scored 40 points and grabbed 17 rebounds, and one of his hoops was a thunderous power dunk over the Knicks' seven-foot center, Patrick Ewing.

It turned out to be a great year for Charles, but not for the Sixers. The team fell to 36-46 and was out of the playoffs. At the same time Charles Barkley became an NBA All-Star. He finished fourth in the league in scoring with a 28.3 average, best of his career. He was sixth in rebounding with 11.9 per game, and third in shooting percentage at 58.7.

He also scored 40 or more points on seven occasions and had 20 or more rebounds four times. He was a starter on the East squad for the All-Star Game for the second straight year. He was an All-League pick and won the Shick Award for the third consecutive season. In the eyes of most he was now in the same class as Magic, Larry, and Michael.

With Charles's star at its zenith, the respect for his overall game continued to grow. Portland coach Rick Adelman said that Charles's court intelligence was underrated. "He's smart in the way he attacks the ball on the offensive glass," Adelman said. "He doesn't get called for many fouls going for the ball, and he doesn't deserve many."

But for Charles the bottom line was winning. "I'm on a mission," he said. "I want to prove I'm a winner. I couldn't do it before with the players we had, but I can do it now. It's put up or shut up time in Philadelphia."

The Sixers rebounded to a 46-36 mark, second in the division to the New York Knicks. Charles had his usual outstanding season—seventh in scoring, second in rebounding, second in field goal percentage. But there was still no title in the cards.

A year later the ball club won the division with a 53-29 mark, but again no title. Then things began going downhill. First came a 44-38 record in 1990–91, then a 35-47 mark the following year. Charles now felt the team was more interested in cutting costs than in winning a championship. The relationship between Charles and management was souring.

In 1991–92 Charles averaged 23.1 points and 11.1 rebounds. He was second team All-NBA, and his 58.0 career field goal percentage was third best on the all-time NBA list. But it was beginning to look as if his days in Philadelphia were numbered. He even began lobbying for a trade.

Then in mid-June of 1992 the deal was made. Charles was sent to the Phoenix Suns in return for guard Jeff Hornacek, center Andrew Lang, and forward Tim Perry. The Suns were an outstanding team. They had a 53-29 record in 1991–92, having lost in the second round of the playoffs to the Portland Trail Blazers. The Suns felt it needed that one big guy to take them over the top.

Charles was overjoyed. "It's all a question of being appreciated," he said. "I just spoke the truth. Reporters asked me about our team, and I said that we didn't have the talent to win. But they were trying to make me out to be a bad guy. That's what I resented."

Before reporting to the Suns, Charles had another stop to make. He joined the Dream Team, the first team of NBA stars allowed to participate in the Olympics. All the big names were there—Jordan, Johnson, Bird, Ewing, Mullin, Malone, Robinson. It was without a doubt the most powerful Olympic basketball team of all time.

They would win the gold medal in a walk. They were the most sought after and popular athletes at the Olympics. Charles ended up the leading scorer on the American team with a 21.6 average. Brazilian star Oscar Schmidt, a fine player in his own right, summed things up when asked about Charles. "We just don't see any like that," Schmidt said.

With his gold medal, Charles reported to the Suns for the first time. Phoenix had some fine players, like guards Kevin Johnson, Dan Majerle, and Danny Ainge, forwards Richard Dumas, Cedric Ceballos, and Tom Chambers. One weakness was center, where Mark West and Oliver Miller didn't score much. Barkley would provide more scoring and a much needed presence on the boards.

From almost the first game of the 1992–93 season

the Suns looked like the best team in the NBA. Charles not only blended in with his new teammates, he became their leader and began putting together the most brilliant season of his career. He topped the team in both scoring and rebounding. And with point guard Kevin Johnson injured a good part of the year, Charles led the team in assists.

When the regular season ended, the Suns had a 62-20 record, the best in basketball. Charles finished fifth in scoring with a 25.6 average, sixth in rebounding at 12.2 a game. He led the Suns in assists with 385. Next came the playoffs; the Suns didn't find it easy.

In the first round the Suns had to work to defeat the Lakers, three games to two. Next they topped San Antonio in six games. But in the conference finals against Seattle, they had to go the full seven games. It was a tired team that took the court against Michael Jordan and the Chicago Bulls for the NBA crown.

Against the Bulls, the Suns looked sluggish in the first two games at home. They lost both. In game two, Charles hit the floor hard and bruised his shooting elbow severely. Thirty minutes before game three it had to be drained of fluid.

That game was a barn burner. It went to triple overtime before Phoenix triumphed, 129–121. Despite his painful elbow, Charles had 24 points and 19 rebounds. But with Michael Jordan playing at his usual super-human level, it was the Bulls who finally won the title in six games, taking the finale, 99–98.

It was a bitter disappointment for Phoenix and Charles. He averaged 27.3 points in the final series and led all rebounders with 78. But Jordan averaged 41 points a game and pulled his team along to their third straight.

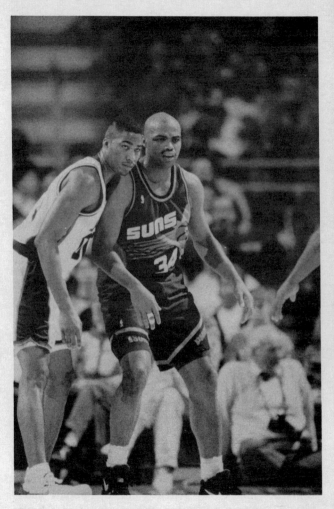

As soon as he joined the suns, Charles became the team's top scorer and rebounder, as well as a floor leader. Now his one wish is to help Phoenix win the NBA championship. *(John Biever photo)*

Shortly after the season, Charles finally got the recognition he so clearly deserved: he was named the NBA's Most Valuable Player for 1992–93. Now his only goal was a world title.

Phoenix was expected to challenge for the title in 1993–94 again, but it would be a tough year for Charles and his teammates. Several players were hurt, and Charles was plagued by a chronically bad back. He would miss 17 games.

He knew that the great Larry Bird had been forced to retire because his back pain was so bad. Basketball just wasn't fun when the pain was always there. It was reflected in Charles's final stats. The Suns finished with a 56-26 mark, six games behind the previous year and second to Seattle (63-19) in the Pacific Division.

In 65 games Charles averaged just 21.6 points a game and 11.2 rebounds. His other numbers were also down. His shooting percentage was just 49.5 percent. That was far from vintage Barkley. Now the team could only hope to rebound in the playoffs.

The Suns won the first two games of their opening best of five against the Golden State Warriors. Then in the third game a national television audience saw Charles Barkley put on a performance that will be remembered for a long time.

Charles came out blazing. He was hitting three-pointers, turnaround jumpers, and dunks. He made his first 11 field goal tries and at the end of the first quarter had 27 points. By halftime he had 38. He had to keep shooting in the second half because the Warriors kept the game close. When it ended, Phoenix had a 140–133 victory to sweep the series. And Charles Barkley had scored an incredible 56 points.

He had hit on 23 of 31 from the field and 7 for 9

from the line. He also had 14 rebounds. With the exception of a 63-point effort by Jordan several years earlier, it was the most points anyone had scored in the playoffs since 1962. Charles's performance left everyone in awe.

"When he is like that, you can triple-team and it doesn't do anything," said Warrior rookie Chris Webber. "He is the heart and soul of the Phoenix team."

But Charles paid a price: he aggravated the bulging disk in his back and had muscle spasms during the second half.

"I've got to go see the doctor," he said afterward. "I don't feel so good right now."

That left a question mark as the Suns prepared for their next series, a best of seven against the powerful Houston Rockets, led by center Hakeem Olajuwon, who would succeed Charles as the league's MVP.

The first two games were in Houston, and suddenly it looked as if the Suns had regained the magic. They won both, 91–87 and 124–117 in overtime. Now the home court advantage was theirs, and Charles was playing well, though he was still in pain. But then the tables turned. Houston won the next two at Phoenix, then the fifth back home for a 3–2 lead.

Charles had scored 30 in the losing fifth game, but got very little scoring support as the rest of the team managed only 56 more points. The Suns rallied for a 103–89 win at home in game six, then headed back to Houston for the deciding seventh game.

In this one Charles's injuries caught up with him. His back pain was severe, but he played as long and as hard as he could. In the end, Houston won it, 104–94, despite 24 points and 15 rebounds by Charles in a courageous performance.

"I think the best team won this series," a gracious Charles said. "I'm still very proud of our team."

Charles had averaged 27.6 points in 10 playoff games despite his injuries. But it was clear that playing in pain was on his mind. "The bottom line is I'm not going to play in pain again like I have this year," he said. "I don't think any human should be taking injections into his back. I'm not going to torture myself again. I'm disappointed the way the season ended, but I'm also glad it's over. The final game was a struggle for me. I couldn't run. I couldn't jump. And a couple of times when I tried to make a move, I couldn't move."

Charles said the condition of his back would determine whether he retired or not. During the off-season, he said his therapy was going well and he would return, but back problems can flare up at any time and no one wanted to see a Hall of Fame career end early because of injury.

There is little doubt about Charles Barkley's greatness. He has proved it time and again. And he's survived the off-court controversies that have periodically surrounded him. Unlike many star athletes who rarely go out in public, Charles refuses to closet himself. He wants to enjoy life and enjoy his celebrity. He has made numerous commercials and is one of the most high-profile athletes in the country.

No matter what his public image, those who know him best know the real Charles Barkley. Perhaps teammate Danny Ainge summed it up best: "Charles is the most fun-loving guy I've ever played with," Ainge said. "He reminds me of guys I played with on the Celtics who would have all this fun. But when the game started, they'd be right there. And that's Charles."

PATRICK EWING

THE GREAT NBA CENTER WILT CHAMBERLAIN SAID something that has often been repeated: "Nobody loves Goliath." Wilt was referring to the biblical giant felled by a stone from the sling of the much smaller David. He meant that no one loves the big guy, the center, the dominant player. If he dominates, he's a bully. If his team is beaten, it's his fault; he hasn't lived up to expectations.

Maybe that's oversimplifying the situation. But in the NBA the center carries a huge burden. He's the man who is supposed to lead his team to a championship.

It is the burden of great expectations that has made Patrick Ewing's life in the NBA something less than perfect. The seven-foot center of the New York Knicks has been a great player in the league since his rookie year, 1985–86. Whenever the names of the great centers of the 1980s and 1990s are listed, Ewing is generally mentioned in the same breath with Hakeem Olajuwon, David Robinson, and recently Shaquille O'Neal.

But Ewing seems to come under more criticism than the others. Some people say he's not a true center because he prefers to take 15-foot jump shots instead of going to the hoop. They say he's not a good rebounder for a player with his size and strength. And the unkindest cut of all: his critics point out the fact that he hasn't led his team to a championship.

Whether Ewing eventually goes down in history as one of the top centers of his time or not, one thing cannot be denied: Patrick has worked very hard for everything he has achieved. Nothing came easy.

Patrick Ewing was born on August 5, 1962, in Kingston, Jamaica. In 1971 his mother, Dorothy Phipps Ewing, left Jamaica for the United States. Her husband, Carl, and her seven children stayed behind. Mrs. Ewing looked to America as a place where the family could make a better life. She had a plan and was willing to sacrifice.

She arrived in Cambridge, Massachusetts, where she got a job in the cafeteria at Massachusetts General Hospital. She also rented a five-room apartment. Then she began sending for her children one or two at a time. Her husband came in 1973. Patrick finally arrived in 1975 when he was 12.

Mrs. Ewing always told her children about the value of education. Patrick listened and trusted her completely. When he first came to Cambridge, Patrick needed a tutor to help him with language. Though English is spoken in Kingston, the Jamaican accent can be difficult for Americans to understand. Patrick worked hard, as he did with everything else.

As for basketball, he had never even seen the game played before he came to America. In Jamaica he had been a soccer goalie for a while, but he never really liked the sport. Shortly after he arrived in Cambridge he saw some kids playing basketball and was intrigued.

"I could see the object was to put the ball in the basket," Patrick has said, looking back. "But [the game] was more difficult than I could have imagined."

Patrick's father was 6'2½". None of his brothers or grandparents were any taller. Yet young Patrick began to grow rapidly. He could dunk a ball when he was in the seventh grade, and he was about 6'6" when he started the eighth grade. But the basketball skills came slowly, and he had to work very hard to learn and perfect his game.

He started as a point guard, but that didn't last long. Grow tall and they put you in the middle. So Patrick had to learn a new position and all the moves that went with it. By the time he was in the tenth grade at Rindge & Latin High School in Cambridge he was beginning to show outstanding skills.

That was in the fall of 1978. Mike Jarvis was the coach at Rindge & Latin, and he knew he had found a potential superstar.

Perhaps the best advice during those years came from Patrick's mother. She told her son, "Work hard and do it right or don't do it at all. Let people say or think what they will."

So Patrick began three years of hard work at Rindge & Latin. He worked at his basketball and he worked at his studies, especially reading. Every summer he went to the Upward Bound program at Wellesley College, opting to study instead of attending basketball camp. But during the season he worked, learned, and won.

With Patrick in the middle, Rindge & Latin would win three straight championships and lose just a single game in three years. The big guy would become a prep All-American and finally national high school Player of the Year.

"Patrick took something God gave all of us—potential—and developed it," said Coach Jarvis. "Once you told him something, he never forgot. He never missed a day of practice. Not one. Never did he miss a class or study hall. Nobody received more criticism from the day he started to play. But he just kept on practicing."

He did it despite racial taunts and taunts about his reading ability and his intelligence. But he worked hard at his reading, and when it was time to go to college, he was ready academically.

John Thompson was a former NBA backup center and teammate of Bill Russell with the Celtics. Now he was the coach of the Georgetown Hoyas. When Patrick was in the tenth grade, Thompson saw him play and said immediately, "Get me him and I'll win the national championship."

By his senior year Patrick had become a naturalized United States citizen and was now looking forward to college. He liked the things John Thompson had to say, and the coach agreed that education was just as important as basketball. On February 3, 1981, Patrick signed a letter of intent to attend Georgetown University in Washington, D.C., that fall.

"It wasn't a bad thing for Patrick to have the image of John Thompson to look up to," said Mike Jarvis. "A center. Russell's friend. A great coach. And a black man."

Patrick went to Georgetown with a reputation as the best young big man in the country. The Hoyas had been 20-12 the year before, and with Ewing in the lineup, the team was expected to do even better.

Under John Thompson, the Hoyas played very aggressive basketball. Some criticized Coach Thompson for fostering an us-against-them mentality. But the Hoyas were always a very close-knit group of players who were ready to go to war for one another.

Under the Georgetown system, it wasn't necessary for Patrick to score in big numbers. He wasn't the focal point of the offense. His job was to clog the middle, concentrate on rebounding and blocking shots. If the opportunity to score arose, he took it.

By the time the regular season ended, the Hoyas were 23-6 and ranked in the top ten in all the major polls. Next came the Big East tournament. Georgetown whipped Providence, then St. John's, and finally Villanova to take the tourney and the Big East title. Now it was on to the NCAAs.

The Hoyas were the top seed in the West Region, and they rolled over the competition, topping Wyoming, then Fresno State, and finally fourth-ranked Oregon State, 69–45, to head into the Final Four. With Patrick leading the way, Georgetown was given a good chance to win the national title.

In the semifinals the Hoyas went up against a very solid Louisville team. The game was a defensive battle with Georgetown prevailing, 50–46. Now the club was ready to play for the national championship, but it wouldn't be easy.

Waiting for Georgetown were the North Carolina Tar Heels. Dean Smith's club was led by All-Americans James Worthy and Sam Perkins as well as a talented freshman named Michael Jordan. In the opening minutes of the game, Patrick Ewing let the whole country know what kind of a force he could be. He went after the first four North Carolina shots and blocked them all!

But he was so anxious to excel that each shot was called goaltending. The baskets counted. So the Tar Heels had an 8–0 lead without even putting the ball through the hoop. A few minutes later the Hoyas had closed the gap and the game became a seesaw struggle.

It finally came down to this: Georgetown had a 62–61 lead with less than a minute remaining. Carolina worked the ball carefully. With fifteen seconds left, freshman Jordan got the ball, took a 16-footer from the left baseline, and hit it! That was, in effect, the winning basket. The Hoyas committed a last-second turnover, and Carolina had the title, 63–62.

It was a heartbreaking loss for Georgetown, but Patrick had been brilliant. He had 23 points on 10-for-15 shooting and led both teams with 11 rebounds. After the season he was named to several second and third team All-American squads. There was little doubt that he was already a college superstar.

For the year Patrick had averaged 12.7 points and 7.5 rebounds. He also had 119 blocked shots. A year later, in 1982–83, the Hoyas lost several key players and slumped to 22-10. They lost in the first round of the Big East tournament and the second round of the NCAAs. But Patrick averaged 17.7 points and 10.2 rebounds to become a consensus All-American his sophomore season.

Before the following season, tragedy struck. In September Patrick's beloved mother died suddenly of a heart attack. Patrick took her death very hard and made a solemn promise to get his degree in fine arts with his graduating class. After that, he would never even discuss leaving school early for the NBA.

That season the Hoyas were a powerhouse. The team roared through the regular season, losing only to DePaul and Big East rivals Villanova and St. John's. They then ripped through the Big East tourney and were the number one seed in the West Regional.

Rival Big East coaches felt the big guy would make the difference. "Ewing doesn't just beat you, he tears you apart," said St. John's Louie Carnesecca.

Rollie Massimino of Villanova put it this way: "He's Bill Russell. That's the only comparison I could make."

Sure enough, the Hoyas whipped Southern Methodist, the University of Nevada at Las Vegas, and Dayton to reach the Final Four. Then they topped Kentucky, 53–40, and were in the title game once more. This time they had to face the Houston Cougars and another top center, Hakeem Olajuwon. But the Hoyas' all-around game was too much for Houston. Georgetown led, 40–30, at the half, and cruised to an 84–75 victory—and the national championship.

Patrick had just 10 points and 9 rebounds in the final. But that was all the team needed from him. Georgetown was an all-around power that played a team game. As Kentucky center Mel Turpin said about the Hoyas, "They took everything away from me. Every time I turned around they were in my face."

Patrick had a 16.4 scoring average and 10.0 rebounding mark his junior year, blocking another 133 shots and becoming a consensus All-American selection for the second time. With most of the principal players returning in 1984–85, the Hoyas were favorites to repeat as champs. And Patrick was an odds-on choice to be Player of the Year.

With the exception of a one-point loss to St. John's and a two-point defeat by Syracuse, Georgetown ripped through the schedule with a vengeance to become the top team in the country. They won the Big East Tourney easily, then ran over four more opponents in the NCAA playoffs. When they reached the Final Four there were two other Big East teams waiting—St. John's and Villanova. Memphis State was the fourth.

In the semifinal, the Georgetown defense held St. John's All-American Chris Mullin to 8 points, while Williams had 20 and Ewing 16. Georgetown won, 77–59, and the Hoyas were again in the title game, this time against Villanova. The Wildcats had come into the tourney with a 19-10 record and were the Cinderella team. During the regular season the Hoyas had beaten Villanova twice, but both games had been close.

So was this one. Villanova played an incredible game, a nearly perfect game, beating the Georgetown press and shooting the ball at a record 78.6 percent from the field. Still, the game went down to the wire with the Wildcats hanging on for a 66–64 upset victory.

In his last game for the Hoyas, Patrick had just 14 points and 5 boards. There was little doubt that Georgetown had the better team. It was just one of those incredible nights when it all went right for Villanova. For Patrick and the Hoyas, it had been a great run.

Patrick averaged 14.6 points and 9.2 rebounds in his final season. His 135 blocks gave him 493 for his career. He was a consensus All-American for the third straight season and was named Player of the Year by several organizations. And many still considered him the best potential NBA center to come out of college in years.

His college career over, Patrick praised his coach, John Thompson. "He helped me grow as a person, and nothing could replace that," he said.

Patrick graduated with a B.A. in Fine Arts with his class in the spring of 1985.

"Getting that degree meant more to me than an NCAA title," Patrick said. "I made a promise to my mother before she died, and I'm proud to have fulfilled that promise."

Now it was on to other things. The 1985 NBA draft was the first that used a lottery system. The eligible teams would get their draft position by having team names drawn at random. It was no secret that the team drawing the first position would take Patrick. That team turned out to be the New York Knicks, and they wasted no time in making Ewing the number one pick in the draft.

Though the Knicks were one of the NBA's flagship franchises the team had not won a title since 1973. The year before Patrick's arrival the team had fallen apart and finished with a 24-58 record. The team had a superstar scorer in Bernard King, but he had suffered a career-threatening knee injury in the second half of the 1984–85 season. Talent beyond King was thin. So with the drafting of Patrick Ewing, great expectations began.

Knicks coach Hubie Brown predicted Patrick would "make an immediate impact." He was called everything from "the Franchise Saver" to "Saint Patrick" to "the Second Coming of Bill Russell." A ten-year contract, worth some $31.2 million, showed that the Knicks were also betting on Ewing. The pressure and the spotlight were now unavoidable.

"I don't consider myself a savior," Patrick told the press. "It's nice to be mentioned in the same breath with Bill Russell, but I'm Patrick Ewing, no more and no less. I have my own style of playing."

The first three seasons of the Ewing era in New York didn't help establish Patrick as anything close to a savior. The team just wasn't that good. Patrick sometimes shuttled back and forth between center and power forward when the 7'1" veteran center, Bill Cartwright, was healthy. He also had to battle his own injuries, injuries that limited him to 58 games his rookie season and 63 the next.

He quickly showed he could score in the NBA, putting up averages of 20.0, 21.5, and 20.2 in his first three years. But he never had more than 676 rebounds in any of those campaigns, and strong seven-foot centers are supposed to do much better than that. The Knick record those years was 23-59 and 24-58 under Hubie Brown, then 38-44 under new coach Rick Pitino.

He was good enough to become Rookie of the Year in 1985–86, but he was frequently surly with reporters and often refused interviews. Those who knew him said he was a fun-loving guy, fiercely loyal to his teammates. He also became involved in a New York City Stay-in-School program, but that kind of stuff didn't get the same publicity as refusing an interview.

Then in 1988–89 the team gelled. Power forward Charles Oakley came over from Chicago in a trade for Cartwright. Second-year point guard Mark Jackson ran the offense smoothly, while rookie backup Rod Strickland also showed talent and potential. Gerald

For Patrick Ewing, every game in the NBA is like a war. He goes against the best centers every night and always gives 100 percent in a rough, physical game. *(John Biever photo)*

Wilkins could be an explosive scorer, as could Johnny Newman and Trent Tucker. Pitino preached a pressing, running style of game, and the Knicks became winners again.

The team finished first in the Atlantic Division with a 52-30 record and, while beaten in the second round of the playoffs, seemed headed in the right direction.

Patrick also had his best season to date. He averaged 22.7 points a game and grabbed 740 rebounds. With Oakley a demon on the boards, some of the rebounding pressure was lifted. Ewing also had 281 blocked shots, best of his career. He was third in the league in blocks and fourth in field goal percentage at 56.7 percent. He finished fourth in the MVP balloting. It looked as if he had finally arrived.

In 1989–90 Patino returned to the college ranks to coach at Kentucky, and Stu Jackson was the new Knicks coach. He changed the team's style a bit.

"We made a conscious decision to make Patrick the focal point of the offense," Jackson said. "We wanted to get him the ball more often and in better spots on the floor."

The Knicks got off to a 25–10 start with Patrick looking more and more like the main man.

"He might be the best in the game right now," said Lakers center Mychal Thompson. "He and Magic are shoulder to shoulder."

Though the New York pace finally slowed a bit, the team wound up third in the Atlantic at 45-37. There were still some holes to fill, but Patrick remained consistent, completing his best season ever. He was third in scoring with a 28.2 average, fifth in rebounding at 10.9 per game, sixth in field goal percentage at 55.1, and second in blocked shots with 3.99 per contest.

Once again the team fell short in the playoffs. But now there was optimism for the future.

The team fell back to 39-43 the next season. That was the year the Chicago Bulls began their three-year run as NBA champs. But by 1991–92 it looked as if the Knicks were ready to make a move. Pat Riley was the coach now. He was a proven winner, having taken the L.A. Lakers to four NBA titles in the 1980s.

By this time the Knicks had added the likes of John Starks, Xavier McDaniel, Anthony Mason, and rookie Greg Anthony to the ball club. Riley began teaching a rock-ribbed defense that made the Knicks one of the most physical teams in the league, a tough team to play. The ball club finished the year at 51-31, the same record as Boston in the Atlantic Division.

Patrick had his usual solid year, coming in fifth in scoring (24.0) and eighth in rebounding (11.2). In the playoffs, the club got even closer. This time they reached the Eastern semifinals, losing to the eventual champion Bulls in seven games. Patrick averaged 22.7 points in 12 playoff games. Would 1992–93 be the year?

In the summer of 1992, Patrick was part of the gold medal–winning Dream Team made up of the first NBA players allowed to compete at the Olympics. When he returned, it was announced that the Knicks had given him a contract extension that would pay him some $33 million over the next five years. So he was still considered the team's franchise player.

Then there were some more changes. Veteran point guard Doc Rivers came over as did forward Charles Smith and shooting guard Rolando Blackman. The Knicks were now the best defensive team in the league.

Through it all, Patrick remained the silent warrior. He was out there every night, playing through minor injuries and pain. More and more, he began coming under fire: he didn't rebound enough; he relied too much on 15-foot jumpers and didn't work inside enough. When the Knicks won, it was a team effort. When they lost, the fingers pointed at the big man in the middle. Like Wilt had said, nobody loves Goliath.

The team finished the year at 60-22. Only the Phoenix Suns (62-20) had a better mark. The two-time champion Bulls were 57-25 in the Central Division. Patrick averaged 24.2 points and 12.1 rebounds. Rookie center Shaquille O'Neal of Orlando was now receiving much of the media attention. O'Neal was outgoing, fun-loving, highly visible, and very talkative—all the things Patrick was not.

Patrick wasn't interested in being any of those things. He was just burning to win that elusive NBA title, which meant everything to him.

In the playoffs the Knicks started by whipping Indiana in four games. Next they defeated the young Charlotte Hornets in just five. Finally it was time for another showdown with the Bulls, the team that had eliminated the Knicks the previous two years. The Bulls were going for their third straight title. Led by Michael Jordan, they were always tough to beat.

At first it looked good. The Knicks won the first two at Madison Square Garden and seemed to be on their way to the final round. But in Chicago Stadium the Bulls came back. They won game three, 103–83, and game four, 105–95, to tie the series.

With Chicago's other star, Scottie Pippen, playing brilliantly, the Bulls upset the Knicks in game five, then closed it out in six, 96–88. The Knicks had lost four straight and were eliminated once again.

It was a bitter loss. Patrick had averaged 25.5 points in 15 playoff games. He and Oakley both hit the boards well, yet they were beaten. Even more people began saying that Patrick needed an NBA title to be considered a great center. It seemed that the criticism would never stop.

Through it all, Patrick's work ethic never wavered. He still gave 100 percent every night, his only object to win the game. Whether the criticism bothered him was difficult to say; he never really commented on it. He always remained a tough and reclusive interview.

Jordan's unexpected retirement prior to the 1993–94 season immediately made the Knicks favorites to take the East. So once again the pressure was on. The team was supposed to win this time. But there were troubles from the start.

The Knicks were struggling on offense. Only Patrick and John Starks were providing consistent offensive punch. Then the team lost veteran guard Doc Rivers to a knee injury. They eventually brought in another veteran, Derek Harper, but it would take him time to get used to the system. Starks would then miss some 23 games. Injuries also shelved Charles Smith and shooting guard Hubert Davis for portions of the year.

Patrick had another consistent season, a 24.5 scoring average and 11.2 rebounding mark. He was sixth in scoring, tenth in rebounding, and seventh in blocks. And while he was still the heart of the Knicks, many felt that Olajuwon (in the midst of his finest season), Robinson, and young O'Neal had all moved ahead of him in total skills.

Primarily Patrick was taken to task for relying too

Patrick often relies on one of the best medium-range jump shots in the league, but he can go hard to the hoop as well. *(John Biever photo)*

much on his deadly jump shot and not spending enough time in the middle, driving to the hoop, and going after rebounds. He had finished fourth in the MVP balloting a year earlier and some felt he should win it in 1993–94. But to him, the title was the most important thing.

"I'd definitely love to win the MVP," Patrick admitted. "But as long as we win a championship, that's it. That's what I want. That's what will make me happy."

Despite the problems and injuries, the Knicks finished with a 57-25 record and won their division once again. Only two teams in the league had better marks. New York was rated the top defensive team in the league, but their offense was near the bottom. What Patrick needed was more help in putting the ball in the basket.

In the first round of the playoffs the Knicks had to meet their regional rivals, the New Jersey Nets. The New York defense dominated the series, and the Knicks won it in four games. Now they would have a rematch with the Bulls in the Eastern Conference semifinals. Even without Michael Jordan, Chicago still had a formidable team and quickly showed the Knicks they wouldn't go easily.

New York won the first game, 90–86, with Patrick scoring 18 and getting 12 boards. The second game was also close, but New York prevailed again, 96–91. This time Patrick had 26.

Now the series returned to Chicago. If the Knicks could take the third game the series would be all but over.

Game three was undecided until the last second when Chicago's Toni Kukoc hit the winning shot. When Chicago won the fourth game, 95–83, it was all tied. If it hadn't been for a controversial call at the end of game five that allowed Hubert Davis to sink two last-second free throws for an 87–86 Knicks win, the Bulls would have had the lead. But Chicago stormed back in game six, winning 93–79 and setting up a seventh and deciding game.

Once again the pressure was on Patrick, who had vowed before the playoffs to lead the Knicks to the title. Playing clutch ball before the home fans, the Knicks prevailed, 87–77, in another low-scoring defensive struggle. Patrick had been scoreless in the first half, but in the final two periods he exploded for 18 points and 17 rebounds to propel his team to the victory.

"I tried to stay focused," Patrick said. "Even though I didn't score in the first half, I was doing other things, rebounding and passing."

Next came the Indiana Pacers for the conference title. This one also turned into a battle for survival and once again came down to a seventh game at Madison Square Garden. In fact, the Knicks had to win game six at Indiana to survive. In this one, it was Patrick Ewing who stepped up big time.

Patrick wound up scoring 24 points, grabbed a playoff career best 22 rebounds, led the Knicks with seven assists, and had five blocked shots. He also put the game away with the spectacular follow-up dunk of a missed shot with 26.9 seconds left. The Knicks won it, 94–90, and advanced to the finals.

"I want to be the one to make the big play," Patrick said afterward. "If we lose, I'll get the blame anyway. So let it be because of me."

Coach Riley put it a little differently. "Patrick wants

to win so much that he'll give half of his game away to somebody else in order for them to be successful.''

The final series also promised to be a war. The Knicks would be playing the Houston Rockets, led by the player expected to be the MVP, center Hakeem Olajuwon. Olajuwon and Ewing had met years before in the national title game. That time Ewing and Georgetown had won. Could Ewing and the Knicks do the winning this time?

It turned out to be a strange series, a low-scoring defensive battle that drew the ire of many basketball purists. There were times when neither team seemed to have a clue on offense, the 24-second limit often expiring before the ball could be put up.

The series opened in Houston with the Rockets taking an 85–78 win in a game that was anything but pretty. The Knicks evened things in game two, 91–83. Then both teams traveled to New York for the next three contests. The third game followed the pattern, low scoring and mistake filled, but the Rockets won, 93–89.

In game four the Knicks again rallied to win, 91–82. Then came the pivotal fifth game, the final one at the Garden. The Knicks really needed it. Again they rallied in the fourth quarter for a 91–84 victory. They were now one game away from the title.

Patrick still wasn't shooting well, but his defense was outstanding. In one sequence he blocked a dunk attempt by Houston's Otis Thorpe. Thorpe got the ball back and tried to lay it in, but Ewing got that one, too.

In game six it was Houston and Olajuwon who made the key shots. In the final seconds Starks tried a three-pointer that would have won it all for the

Knicks. But Olajuwon got a piece of it and the ball fell short.

The Rockets' center finished with 30 points, while Starks had 27 for the Knicks. Patrick had just 17, hitting just 6 of 20 from the field and failing to score in the fourth quarter. He did lead everyone with 15 rebounds, however. Now it was down to a single game for the title.

Patrick was taking a lot of heat because of his poor shooting. He felt it was time to point out a few other things about his game. "Everybody's been making a big thing about my scoring," he said, "but I think I'm playing a solid all-around game. I'm rebounding, I'm blocking shots, I'm playing great defense."

That was true, but Olajuwon was doing the same. Perhaps the supporting cast would decide the final game.

The seventh game was like all the others, close from start to finish. The Rockets led by one at the quarter, by two at the half, and by three at the end of three. So it all came down to the final 12 minutes. For the Knicks, shooting was the key again. Starks, who had the hot hand in game six, suddenly went ice cold and would wind up just 2 for 18 from the field. Patrick was just 7 for 17. Yet the game was up for grabs till the very end.

The Rockets emerged with a 90–84 victory and the NBA championship. Olajuwon had 25 points, a title, and the MVP prize. For Patrick and the Knicks there was only bitter disappointment.

"I'm extremely disappointed in the fact that we didn't win a championship, but I still feel proud of my teammates," Patrick said. "I thought we gave 110 percent, and unfortunately it wasn't enough to get the win."

In a strange way the championship round may have earned Patrick more respect. People have always focused on his scoring, on his jump shooting. Though his shots didn't fall in so often in the final round, Patrick didn't quit. He rebounded, blocked shots, and played defense better than ever before. Is he the best? Maybe not.

But he's darn close.

CHRIS MULLIN

OVERCOMING OBSTACLES SEEMS TO BE A NATURAL part of Chris Mullin's life. And he's done it the old-fashioned way, by a combination of hard work and a strong will. Nothing has come easy for the 6'6" forward/guard of the Golden State Warriors. In fact, Mullin may be the most unlikely superstar in the entire NBA.

Chris Mullin is a veteran player, a former college basketball Player of the Year, an All-American, a two-time Olympic gold medal winner, and an NBA All-Star. Yet he has always been considered a slow guy who can't jump and who isn't as strong as many other players.

He's also had to make adjustments. Chris had to change his game after going from St. John's University to the Warriors. And even more difficult for him was overcoming alcoholism, an illness he talks openly about in the hope of helping others.

Chris Mullin was born on July 30, 1963, in Brooklyn.

One of five children born to Rod and Eileen Mullin, Chris often shared a bedroom with his three brothers, Roddy, John, and Terence, while growing up; older sister Kathy had her own room. The family lived two blocks from St. Thomas Aquinas Church, where they went to mass every Sunday.

Basketball was a big part of Chris's life from his earliest days. Shooting the ball into the basket was something he could always do and always wanted to do better. When he was in the fourth grade, Chris entered a national free-throw shooting contest, traveling to Kansas City, Missouri, for the finals. Even with the pressure on, he sank 23 of 25 shots to take the championship.

When he was 12, Chris attended Lou Carnesecca's summer basketball camp. Carnesecca was the longtime coach at St. John's University in Brooklyn. Louie saw even then that this local kid had a passion for the game matched by very few others.

When he was ready for high school Chris decided to follow brother Roddy to Power Memorial, the school where Lew Alcindor (later known as Kareem Abdul-Jabbar) first came to national attention. At Power, Chris helped lead the freshman and jayvee teams to the New York City championship. He seemed to be on his way.

But then in his junior year Chris ran into a major obstacle. After joining the varsity, he found himself playing for a coach who allegedly had had a "personality conflict" with his brother Roddy. When Chris felt his brother's problem spilling over on him, he decided to transfer to Xaverian High. The school rules stated that because he transferred in January, Chris had to sit out the final half of his junior year and almost half of his senior season the following fall. Sitting out hurt. "I knew it was a risky move," he said. "For a while I was afraid that nobody [from the colleges] would see me. And it really hurt me not to play ball."

As usual, Chris took the time to work hard at his game. Xaverian assistant coach Jack Alesi, who had known Chris since elementary school days, says the youngster "trained like a prizefighter" so he would be ready for the final half of his senior year.

Chris's first game with Xaverian was against Christ the King High with some 1,000 fans packed into the small gym. He scored 17 of his team's first 21 points and finished with a sensational 38 for the night. Since high school games are just 32 minutes long, that averages out to more than a point a minute.

Not surprisingly, Chris's outstanding play led Xaverian to the state championship in its division. The next logical question was where he would go to college. There were certainly enough major schools that would want the talented kid from Brooklyn, but it wasn't a campus that Chris wanted. He wanted to stay in Brooklyn.

"I wasn't looking for grass and nice buildings," he said. "A dorm school has more distractions. At St. John's I was still close to my neighborhood, could live at home, study, and play ball."

It was the fall of 1981 when Chris Mullin entered St. John's. Once basketball started, he quickly showed how well he would fit in. Coach Carnesecca was impressed from the outset. "The first game Mo [Chris's nickname] played here, it was as if he had been here at St. John's for a hundred years," the veteran coach said.

Chris wasn't about to rest on his laurels, however.

He had a well-established routine. After school and practice were over, he'd head home for dinner. Then he would take care of his studies before heading back to the gym at Alumni Hall, where he would shoot the basketball until he got tired.

The hard work paid off. St. John's finished the 1981–82 season with a 21-9 mark, and Chris finished as the team's second leading scorer with 498 points for a 16.6 average. He was also second in assists with 92 and tied for first in steals with 43. Against other teams in the very tough, very physical Big East Conference, he averaged 18.2 points a game and made a number of all-freshman all-star teams.

In 1982–83, Chris emerged as the St. John's team leader. The ball club was outstanding that year, and Mullin more and more began to resemble an unlikely superstar. Some people complained that he was a tad slow, wasn't a great leaper, and should be physically stronger. But his choirboy appearance was deceiving. He was tough as nails underneath, with a will to win and excel that matched that of any player in the land.

"Mo makes everything look so easy," said Coach Carnesecca. "But it's all happened before, over and over. He sees plays before they develop. He photo-flashes them and then creates. I watch him and I see Joe DiMaggio in center field. I learn from Mo."

Chris could play both shooting guard and small forward with equal ease, often swinging back and forth between the two positions in the same game. With several other outstanding players, the Redmen put together a great year and were in the top ten almost the entire season. They wound up the third-ranked team in the country in both the AP and UPI final polls.

The biggest disappointment was losing to Georgia

At St. John's, Chris wasn't considered very fast. But he already had the knack of faking defenders off their feet. *(Courtesy St. John's University)*

in the East Regionals of the NCAA tournament. But the club's 28-5 record was one of its best ever, and Chris Mullin played a huge role in that achievement.

He led the team in scoring with 629 points and a 19.1 average. In addition, he shot an impressive 57.7 percent from the field and 87.8 from the foul line. All his other numbers were up, and on March 5 he became the third player in school history to score 1,000 points in just two seasons. He was also named Big East Player of the Year and was named a second team All-American by *Basketball Times*.

In his junior year, Chris was still an improving player. And on the night of February 21, 1984, he gave his greatest performance yet against Big East rival Georgetown University.

He played an incredible game on both offense and defense. Then the game came down to the final seconds. The Redmen were leading by two, but Georgetown had the ball. Suddenly Chris was there, stealing the ball from Horace Broadnax and feeding Mark Jackson for a breakaway jam that put the game on ice. The Redmen won it, 75–71, for their biggest victory of the year.

And all Chris Mullin did was hit on 13 of 18 shots from the field and 7 of 8 from the line for 33 points. He also had four assists, three steals, and four rebounds in a virtuoso performance.

"The way Chris played against Georgetown, it was almost like the ball was on a string in his hand," said teammate Ron Stewart. "He gave us three times our usual confidence. We saw him going, so everybody just went with him."

As Coach Carnesecca said, "The good players make

themselves better. The great players make others better."

St. John's finished the season with an 18-12 record, losing to Temple in the first round of the NCAA tournament. But Chris had a tremendous year, averaging 22.9 points a game, hitting 57.1 percent of his shots from the field and an amazing 90.4 from the free throw line. He was named to the first and second teams of a number of All-American squads and also shared with Ewing the prize for Big East Player of the Year.

That summer Chris was a member of the United States Olympic team, which won a gold medal in Los Angeles. His 93 points in eight games was second only to Michael Jordan. Yet he wasn't a starter and was fifth on the team in minutes played.

Back at St. John's for his senior year, Chris was ready for an All-American season. This time he had a very good supporting cast that included junior-college transfer Walter Berry, a rugged forward with All-American potential.

It didn't take the Redmen long to begin winning and to establish themselves as a national power. A midseason 66–65 upset of defending national champ Georgetown made St. John's the number one team in the country for a time.

Coming into the Big East tournament the Redmen had lost only two games. But then they were beaten by Georgetown, sending them to the West Regional of the NCAA tournament. There they swept the West to reach the coveted Final Four. Also coming to the Rupp Arena in Lexington, Kentucky, were two other Big East teams—defending champ Georgetown and upstart Villanova. The fourth club was Memphis State.

There was little doubt that the Hoyas had the most

talent, especially with Ewing in the middle. Unfortunately, St. John's had to meet them in the semifinals. A combination of the stingy Georgetown defense and perhaps an old-fashioned off day held Chris to just eight points. Georgetown won easily, 77–59, eliminating the Redmen once more.

Nonetheless, it had been a fine year for Chris and his team. The ball club was 31-4 for the season and ranked number three in the land. Chris had also emerged as the leading scorer in the NCAA tournament with 110 points in five games. For the year he had averaged 19.8 points, and he had a career best 169 rebounds plus 151 assists, 73 steals, and 17 blocked shots.

He ended his St. John's career as the school's all-time leading scorer with 2,440 points and a 19.5 average. This time he was a consensus All-American selection and, better yet, the winner of the John Wooden Award as college basketball's Player of the Year.

With Chris's skills and credentials, it seemed the next logical step would be the NBA. On draft day Chris waited anxiously. The best scenario for him would have been getting drafted by the New York Knicks. That way he could have stayed home, close to family, friends, and his girlfriend from St. John's. But unfortunately, players don't have control of the draft.

The Knicks did have the first pick that year, but they opted for Patrick Ewing of Georgetown. So Chris had to wait, but not for long. The seventh pick belonged to the Golden State Warriors, and they wasted no time in making Chris their first-round selection.

Chris would have to travel 3,000 miles from home

to play pro basketball in California for a team that had lost 60 games the year before. Needless to say, he was not overjoyed. Maybe that was why he held out until he got the contract he wanted. He didn't sign until November 6, inking a four-year deal after he missed the entire preseason and six games of the regular season.

At Golden State he also found a number of players who didn't have his work ethic, but he joined the team and began seeing considerable action. Statistically it looked like a pretty good rookie year. Chris played in 55 games, then missed the final 20 with a heel injury. He averaged 14 points a game, but only had 115 rebounds. He still managed 70 steals and 23 blocks. And his 89.6 free throw percentage was the second best for a rookie in NBA history. He appeared to have the makings of a solid role player, maybe a sixth man type, but certainly not a superstar.

The Warriors were just 30-52 and last in 1985–86. That was another adjustment for Chris, used to playing on winning teams. No one really knew it then, but he had begun to adopt a lifestyle that would soon reach crisis proportions. While he started all 82 games the following year and averaged 15.1 points a game, Chris was still not the dominant player he had been in college. The team was 42-40 and in the playoffs, but Chris averaged just 11.3 points in 10 playoff games with 23 rebounds. Again, not winning numbers.

Chris was very lonely in California and missed his friends and family. He had always enjoyed a few beers with his friends after games or after his long practice sessions back in Brooklyn. But now he was drinking too much, and that began to affect his life, his work ethic, and his game.

When he went home that summer, the people closest to him saw the change. His father, Rod, had had an alcohol problem, but had stopped drinking in 1980. He knew there was only so much he could say to his son.

"How can you tell the Wooden Award winner, the Player of the Year, an All-American, that he can't drink?" Rod Mullin once said.

Chris reported to the Warriors for his third season in the fall of 1987. Now it was more apparent than ever that he had a problem. His play early in the season wasn't good. He wasn't really helping the team.

Finally, in early December, Coach Nelson decided to have a frank talk with Chris. The coach didn't mince words. "You've got a drinking problem," he said flat out.

Chris denied it at first, but he accepted the coach's challenge to prove it by not drinking for two months. The two shook hands. Then, two nights later, someone told Nelson that Chris had been drinking at a local bar. On December 10 Nelson suspended Mullin for missing two practices, and two days later he put Chris on the injured list.

The two then had another talk. "I want you to take care of this problem right now," the coach ordered his player. "Call your parents and your agent."

That's when Chris decided he needed help. On December 12 he checked into a rehabilitation clinic and so informed his family and friends. They were all happy that he would be getting help.

"It was easy to look around at the others in there and say, 'Hey, you're messed up, not me,'" Chris admitted. "But then I remembered that my dad always said that you can always take the easy way out, but the easy way is usually the wrong way."

That was a turning point. Chris was at the clinic for more than a month and away from the team for a month and a half. When he rejoined the Warriors he had missed 22 games. Since then, he has always credited Don Nelson as the man who turned it around. "He might have saved my life," Chris said.

In his first informal workout after rehab, Chris made 91 straight free throws. He still had the eye, but the question now was could he develop an NBA-caliber game? He wound up with a 20.5 average in 60 games, the best mark of his career. His rebounds and steals were also up. But he was far from satisfied. His drinking problem behind him, Chris went back to work with his former zeal, determined to regain his status as a premier player.

During his first three years Chris had been described as a catch-and-shoot player who didn't have a lot of moves, was weak on defense, and simply didn't create enough or have enough of an all-around game. Even Don Nelson had admitted he was disappointed.

"I heard he was so good," Nelson said. "But he wasn't. He had a drinking problem and was overweight, and I wasn't pleased with him on defense."

During the off-season Chris embarked on a routine to toughen both his body and mind for the next NBA season. It was a routine that would become his norm, a workout schedule so difficult that people worried he would burn himself out. It went something like this:

Chris would get up at about 6:30 A.M. and run five miles. When he returned from the run, he would spend an hour on a stair-climber exercise machine at a high setting. After that it was on to a stationary bike for yet another hour. Then came a swim in the pool and a break for lunch. After lunch he worked out in the weight room for about an hour and a half. Then came gym time. He would shoot about 400 jumpers in a half hour, then shoot some 200 free throws to end the day. He did this nearly every day during the off-season.

When Chris rejoined the Warriors for the 1988–89 season he was a different player. His body, once described as lumpy, was now hard and taut. His stamina was incredible, and his skill level had moved up several notches in every area of the game. Though he still couldn't be called fast, he knew how to get open and could get off his smooth-as-silk jumper in a crowd or while being bumped or jostled.

"Chris is one of the best I've ever seen at taking the hit and still finishing the shot," said teammate Rod Higgins.

Chris would have team conditioning coach Mark Grabow push and shove him during his shooting drills. That way he worked on keeping both his balance and his concentration while finishing a shot.

The result was that Chris became an instant All-Star. He wound up the season as the fifth best scorer in the league, averaging 26.5 points for all 82 games. He shot 50.9 percent from the field and 89.2 percent from the free throw line. But that wasn't all. He more than doubled his rebounds, getting 483, had a career best 415 assists and a career best 176 steals. He also became the third player in Warrior history—joining all-time greats Wilt Chamberlain and Rick Barry—to get more than 2,000 points, 400 rebounds, and 400 assists in the same season.

After the season, he was named to the All-NBA

second team. One of his best games ever came on April 13, 1989, when he scored a career high 46 points in an overtime game against the L.A. Clippers. And after seeing the much-improved Mullin, the Warriors gave him a new nine-year contract that would run right through the 1997–98 season.

Once he emerged as an NBA star, Chris never looked back. He continued his brutal off-season workouts.

Sometimes his coach worried that he worked too hard. "I can't tell you that I don't worry about him burning out," said Don Nelson. "Most athletes have a hard day and then a rest day. Chris has a hard day and then a harder day. Followed by another hard day."

But Chris's mental attitude had changed along with his approach to the game. "I don't get as upset by a bad game anymore," he said. "That's all it is—a bad game. It's funny. Basketball doesn't mean as much to me now, but at the same time I'm more dedicated to it."

In 1989–90 Chris led the Warriors in both scoring and rebounding, though the team missed the play-offs—they still had no big center. But even losing didn't keep Chris from playing his best every night.

The next year he averaged 25.7 points a game while shooting 53.6 percent from the field and 88.4 percent from the line. No player in league history had ever posted a higher-scoring average while shooting better field goal and free throw percentages. He was named a starter in the All-Star Game for the first time and was once again named an All-NBA second teamer.

Then in 1991–92, after another brilliant season, he was finally named to the All-NBA first team. In addition to his usual outstanding statistics, he also led the league for a consecutive second year in minutes

An NBA All-Star throughout the 1990s, Chris has one of the quickest and deadliest jump shots in the entire league. *(Courtesy Golden State Warriors)*

played. All that extra work and conditioning allowed him to go all out for more minutes than anyone else.

"He's been truly remarkable," said Coach Nelson. "He's a superstar. There's no question anymore in anyone's mind."

But maybe it was former Chicago Bulls coach Doug Collins who best caught the essense of what Chris Mullin had become. "The rap against Mullin is that he's too slow," said Collins. "If that's true, isn't it funny how nobody can guard him, that he can get off a shot—whether from the outside or the post area— against any defender? When he misses an open shot, it's cause for surprise. If I had to pick one guy to attempt the last shot with the game on the line, Mullin would be my choice."

In the summer of 1992 Chris was a member of the United States Dream Team, the first group of NBA stars allowed to compete in the Olympic Games. Playing alongside the likes of Michael Jordan, Charles Barkley, Hakeem Olajuwon, Magic Johnson, Larry Bird, and Patrick Ewing, Chris averaged 12.9 points a game while shooting an amazing 61.9 from the field. The United States easily won the gold medal, and Chris became the second-leading all-time scorer in Olympic competition, behind Jordan. The one disappointment in Chris's tenure with the Warriors was that Golden State still hadn't become one of the NBA's elite teams.

In 1992–93 Chris was again having a typical Mullin season. After 41 games, he was averaging a career best 26.7 points, including a big 46-point effort against Charlotte. Then, in the team's forty-second game, he tore the collateral ligament in his right thumb. Chris played in four more games. But with his effectiveness cut severely, he opted for immediate surgery. He would miss the final thirty-six games of the year.

The next year would turn into a crossroads. There was a high for everyone early on when the draft produced Michigan's Chris Webber, a 6'10" forward/center of enormous skill and potential. Webber just might be the big man the Warriors had been seeking for more than a decade.

But then the injury jinx hit once again. Before the season even began, the Warriors lost All-Star guard Tim Hardaway for the season, valuable swingman Sarunas Marciulionis, also for the season, and Chris Mullin to yet another ligament injury in his right hand. Of the three, Chris's injury was the least serious.

Webber would end up Rookie of the Year and had the makings of an outstanding player, the big man the Warriors hadn't had since Chris joined the team. Chris, however, would miss the first twenty games of the year before rejoining the ball club.

After missing most of the final half of the previous season and first quarter of the current one, his timing and his shooting were off. They returned slowly. The team was playing an exciting brand of basketball and winning, though. Before long, Chris began putting together some fine games, though his scoring was still down.

Against Seattle on January 14 he scored 18 points and had 12 rebounds and 10 assists (a triple double) as the Warriors won, 121–100, against the team with the best record in the NBA. In a 120–107 victory over powerful Phoenix on March 3, Chris hit 11 of his 13 field goal tries and finished with 25 points, 8 assists, and 7 rebounds. His season high of 32 points came on April 18 against the Clippers. He was still capable of dominating a game.

The Warriors finished the year third in the Pacific Division behind Seattle and Phoenix, but their 50-32 record was 16 games better than it had been the year before. Chris wound up averaging 16.8 points in 62 games, well below his norm. But with Latrell Sprewell scoring 21 a game, rookie Webber 17.5, and Billy Owens 15, the team had better balance. Though they lost in the first round of the playoffs to Phoenix in four games, their future looked bright.

For Chris it had been a rough couple of years. First he had to battle to reach the top of his profession, working as hard as any athlete ever had. Then he had to come back from a number of injuries. In addition, the loss of both parents within three years of each other affected him deeply because the Mullin family had always been so close. His mother's death coincided with his return from injury in 1994.

"I tried to fill the void with basketball, and it didn't work," he admitted. "The first few games back, I thought there would be one game that I would put my stamp on, and everything would get better. Then I realized that wasn't going to happen. I realized there aren't enough jump shots in the world that can make the pain go away. I just have to cry, laugh, see it through."

Now married and with two small children of his own, Chris Mullin has gradually learned that there is more to life than basketball. Yet this knowledge has also made him a better player—in fact, one of the very best. Maybe his father, Rod Mullin, said it best during the final stages of his illness.

"Before he died, he told me he wasn't worried about me anymore," Chris said. "When he left, he said, 'You're gonna be okay. You got the program down.'"

There is no better way to say it.

SCOTTIE PIPPEN

THE SHADOWS CAST BY SPORTS HEROES CAN BE IM-
mense. Sometimes, even after an athlete goes away,
his shadow remains. That may be what has happened
to Scottie Pippen. He has spent his entire career in a
shadow cast by one of the biggest stars in sports.

Scottie is the talented forward/guard of the Chicago
Bulls, a man who helped the Bulls win three straight
NBA titles from 1991 to 1993, who has been a second
team all-NBA selection, a multi-time NBA All-Defensive Team choice, and one of the best all-around players in the game.

The athlete casting the shadow is Michael Jordan,
a man almost unanimously acclaimed as the best
player in the entire history of the game. While Pippen
was becoming a star, Jordan was already *the* superstar.
As Pippen assumed an increasingly large role in his
team's success, the Bulls were still considered Michael's team.

The shadow didn't go away even after the superstar

had disappeared. Jordan's sudden and unexpected retirement prior to the 1993–94 season seemed to free Scottie Pippen to become the leader. Yet the comparisons never stopped. What if Michael had been here? Michael could have done it better. The Bulls wouldn't have lost if Michael was still here.

Michael was gone, but his shadow remained. That was something Scottie Pippen had to deal with—and it wasn't always easy.

Scottie Pippen, to begin with, was an unlikely superstar, one of the long shots who came from nowhere. Unlike Jordan, who was a superstar in college, Scottie came to the Bulls without superstar status. In fact, he could easily have slipped through the cracks and perhaps never achieved the lofty status he holds today.

Scottie was a small-town kid, born on September 25, 1965, in Hamburg, Arkansas. As the youngest of 12 children, he had to compete early just to keep up. His father worked long hours in a paper plant to support his family, while Scottie's mother had the job of raising the kids.

Hamburg had a population of less than 3,500 and had never sent one of its kids to the NBA. And in those early years, no one thought Scottie Pippen would be a future NBA player, either.

"We used to play at the Pine Street courts," said boyhood friend Ron Martin. "When we were 13 or 14 we would play as late as we could, until we were run off for making too much noise. And we'd play everything.

"We would play one-on-one basketball forever, and we were convinced that one of us was going to make the NBA. We just didn't know which one. I was a little bigger than him, heavier and stronger, so I used to lean on him. Then . . . he got big on me."

That didn't happen overnight. When Scottie reached Hamburg High School he was a good athlete and a quiet kid. Nothing exceptional. In fact, when he began his senior year he was just 6'1½" tall and the starting point guard on the team. Ron Martin was still a little bigger and shooting guard.

His coach, Donald Wayne, remembers Scottie as simply a solid player. "He was good, but nothing tremendous," Wayne said. "A consistent player, but not a flashy one."

None of the colleges rushed to Hamburg to scout or recruit young Pippen, but Scottie wanted to go to college, so he asked his coach for help. Coach Wayne called an old friend, Don Dyer, who was the head basketball coach at the University of Central Arkansas in Conway. Wayne told Dyer that he had a point guard who might not be good enough to make the team, but who would make a good team manager under a work-study program. Dyer decided to take a chance.

That was when Scottie Pippen began to grow. He was 6'3" when he arrived at the Conway campus in the fall of 1983.

When the basketball season started, Scottie was handing out the shirts and socks, doing the things a manager was supposed to do. But he also practiced with the team, and before long the team manager was showing skills superior to some of the players. Scottie played twenty games as a skinny freshman, coming off the bench and averaging 4.3 points a game. Sure, he was a college player, but there were still few indications that he was going to be anything more.

By his sophomore year, however, he was up to 6'5" and 165 pounds. He became a starter and averaged 18.5 points and 9.2 rebounds in 19 games. Better, but still no cause to celebrate.

By his junior year, in 1985–86, Scottie was up to 6'6" and a solid 185 pounds. Now he was beginning to look like a player. Arch Jones, an assistant coach at UCA, remembers: "Scottie surprised me in that he never lost any of his coordination in all of his rapid growing. He was always able to take the skills he had learned when he was smaller and use them when he was bigger. His arms were so long and his hands so big that he really played like someone 6'10" or 6'11"."

That was when Scottie Pippen began coming of age. He could do many things on the court—handle the ball, pass, shoot from the outside, or penetrate, play defense, and rebound. These were all skills that he would soon take to the NBA.

As a junior he averaged 19.8 points and 9.2 rebounds. He shot 55.6 percent from the field. But because he played for a small school, not too many people noticed, even when he began making some NAIA All-American teams. So when he began his final year at 6'7" and playing better than ever, he still didn't think much about an NBA future.

That year, 1986–87, Scottie averaged 23.6 points and 10 rebounds. He shot 59.2 percent from the field, including an impressive 57.5 percent (23 of 40) from three-point range. By now there was no denying his skills among small college NAIA players. He became a consensus NAIA All-American. Now the question was whether he had a basketball future.

One of Scottie's biggest supporters was Don Dyer, who had begun feeling Scottie had a chance to make it to the pros at the end of his sophomore season. "I'd seen Sidney Moncrief and Darrell Walker play at the University of Arkansas at the same stage," Dyer side. "They both made it to the NBA. I thought Scottie was bigger and better. So I called San Antonio and Dallas, but no one seemed interested."

The next step for Scottie was to attend some NBA-sponsored tryout camps. He went to one in Chicago where Jerry Krause, the Bulls' GM, took note of his name and then saw him at one of the tryout camps. "Before he even shot the ball I noticed him," Krause said. "He had the longest arms I'd ever seen. I've always been very big on long arms and big hands. I said, 'There's something special.' Then I looked around. Everyone was murmuring."

By the time the draft rolled around, Jerry Krause knew he wanted Pippen. The Bulls had the eighth pick in the first round in 1987, but Krause worried that might not be high enough. He made a deal with the Seattle Supersonics, who had the fifth pick. Then he waited.

Sure enough, Scottie was still available and Seattle took him. Then the Bulls picked center Olden Polynice, the player Seattle wanted. By day's end the trade had been made. Straight up. Scottie Pippen, who'd been team manager the beginning of his freshman year at Central Arkansas, was now a member of the Chicago Bulls.

All this time the Bulls were Michael Jordan's team. A foot injury kept him out of a large part of the 1985–86 season, but Jordan returned to average 43.7 points in three playoff games.

By now many also considered the Bulls a one-man team. Chicago had had just one winning season since

1976–77. With Jordan averaging a ton of points in 1986–87 the Bulls managed just a 40-42 mark and were eliminated from the playoffs in three straight games. Management was anxious to give Jordan the kind of supporting cast that would take the team to the top.

Along with Scottie, Chicago drafted a 6'10" power forward out of Clemson on the second round. Pippen and Horace Grant would form the nucleus of that elusive supporting cast. But it wouldn't happen overnight. For openers, Scottie missed part of his first preseason because of a contract dispute. Then he had to work his way into the lineup.

He played only about 21 minutes a game as a rookie. But Bulls' assistant coach Phil Jackson said he could already see the skills were there. "You could see the possibilities," said Jackson. "He could rebound yet still dribble the length of the court. He could post up. He had those slashing sorts of moves. You knew he could become a very good player, only you didn't know how good. Those first few years we used him mostly at small forward."

Scottie averaged just 7.9 points a game his rookie year, shooting just 46.3 percent from the field. His 3.8 rebounds a game weren't very impressive, either, but he did have thirty double-figure scoring games. The potential was there. The other rookie, Horace Grant, averaged 7.7 points and 5.5 rebounds.

But the rookies helped. The Bulls surprised everyone with a 50-32 finish in the Central Division, four games behind the Detroit Pistons. Jordan led the league in scoring again and got help from power forward Charles Oakley, guard John Paxson, and center Dave Corzine. They weren't a great team, but they

Scottie Pippen is one of those players who can do everything on the basketball court—run, pass, defend, rebound, handle the ball, and shoot. *(John Biever photo)*

won. In the playoffs, they whipped Cleveland in five games, 3–2, then lost to the powerful Pistons in five, 4–1.

More changes were made. Veteran center Bill Cartwright came over from the Knicks for Charles Oakley. Long-range shooting Craig Hodges also came in a trade, while center Will Purdue of Vanderbilt was the top draft choice. One setback was Scottie Pippen, who needed off-season back surgery. He would miss the entire preseason and first eight games of the regular season.

It wasn't long after he rejoined the team that Scottie became a starter. He was now beginning to show the varied skills that people had seen in him all along. In fact, he was beginning to take his place alongside the amazing Jordan as the team's second best all-around player.

In 73 games in 1988–89 Scottie averaged 14.4 points a game, scoring a high of 31 on two occasions. He also grabbed 445 rebounds, or 6.1 a game, and had 256 assists, 139 steals, and 61 blocked shots. The team finished with a 47-35 record as Jordan took another league scoring title. Their record was good for just fifth place in a very strong Central Division. But they were in the playoffs.

The team really showed it had come of age in the playoffs. First they whipped the Cleveland Cavaliers in five tough games. They then went six before topping the New York Knicks. Now the team went up against the Detroit Pistons for the conference title and a right to go to the championship round.

But the Bulls still had trouble coping with the rough defensive style of the Pistons. In the sixth game, with the Pistons trying to wrap it up, Scottie took a hard elbow to the head from Detroit center Bill Laimbeer in the opening minute. He was unable to return, and the Pistons went on to close out the series and take the NBA crown.

Now the Bulls looked to 1989–90. So did Scottie. Phil Jackson had been elevated to head coach and the team would be satisfied with nothing short of a championship.

General manager Jerry Krause, the man who had drafted Scottie, felt even more strongly about his draft decision. "Scottie is still just scratching the surface of what he can be," said Krause. "I think he'll be a better defensive player, although he's not bad now. I think he'll be a better shooter, although his shooting certainly has improved. You look at him—his tools just stun you. And he's just coming into that age range when players are at the top of their game."

Krause was right. Scottie produced his best season ever. He averaged 16.5 points a game in support of Jordan's league best 33.6. He also nailed 6.7 rebounds and had 211 steals, third best in the league. Jordan, one of the best, had 227 steals. In addition, Scottie led the team with 101 blocked shots. He also joined Michael on the midseason All-Star team. He was doing virtually everything.

Once again the Bulls went all the way to the Eastern Conference finals, where they were again beaten by the Pistons, this time in seven games. It looked as if 1990–91 could be their year. It would also be the year that Jerry Krause's prophecy for Scottie Pippen became reality.

From the beginning of the year it was obvious that the Bulls had moved very close to the head of the class. The ball club had one of the best records in the league all year. Jordan was back in his usual position as the league's top scorer. He was now being called the greatest ever to play the game.

It was apparent that second best was Scottie Pippen. He had moved his scoring average close to the 18-point mark, and he drew many of the top defensive assignments. Filled out to 210 pounds, he could bang underneath as well as fly up and down the court.

Coach Jackson described one way in which Scottie's role had changed and grown. "As more and more teams pressed up," Jackson said, "we began thinking about Scottie as a third ball advancer, an offense that attacked at multiple points. From that position he started being able to take control, to make decisions. He became a bit of everything."

So Scottie was sometimes acting as a point guard as well as a small forward. He soon began putting up superstar numbers. In one game against the Clippers, he finished with 13 points, 13 rebounds, and 12 assists. In NBA jargon that's called a triple double, something only the true superstars achieve, players like Jordan, Magic Johnson, and Larry Bird.

Scottie also explained that he had changed his approach to the game. In the 1990 playoffs he was forced to sit out the final losing game to the Pistons because of a migraine headache. It was determined that his headaches were caused by eyestrain and he started wearing glasses off the court.

He also began preparing differently for games. "I eat my breakfast, then don't eat again until after the game," he explained. "I also make sure I get my sleep. I take a nap in the afternoon of the day of the game. Sometimes I don't sleep, but I relax and visualize the game. I think about who I'm guarding, the things he likes to do. I think it helps."

When the season ended, the Bulls took the Central Division with a 61-21 record. Only the Portland Trail Blazers in the Pacific Division had a better mark at 63-19. Jordan was again the scoring champ, with Scottie chiming in at 17.8 points a game.

But the only thing that really mattered now was the playoffs. First the Bulls swept the Knicks in three games. Then they had to face the Philadelphia 76ers. It was more of the same. They closed out the Sixers in five. For the third straight year they had to meet the Pistons for the conference crown. This time it was no contest. Chicago won in four straight to advance to the NBA finals against the Los Angeles Lakers.

In the final victory over Detroit, the Bulls proved once and for all that they were no longer a one-man team. Jordan led the scorers with 29 points. Scottie was right behind with 23, while Horace Grant had 16, and John Paxson 12.

Even Jordan was overjoyed. "I've got to give so much credit to Scottie Pippen, Horace Grant, and the rest of the supporting cast," he said.

The aging Lakers, still led by Magic Johnson, surprised everyone by winning the first game. But Chicago won the second as Scottie scored 20 points and did a brilliant defensive job on Magic, holding him to just 4-for-13 shooting and 14 points. After that, it looked almost easy. The Bulls ran off three more victories to close out the Lakers in five games. They were champions.

All the Bulls were jubilant. They had wanted a title for the team and for the city of Chicago. Scottie Pippen said, "I needed a championship. I needed a chance to prove that I was a money ballplayer."

He would prove it again and again over the next two seasons. During that time the Bulls remained the class of the league. And in 1991–92, Scottie Pippen finally became an acknowledged superstar in his own right, a player so good in so many areas that some people said he was the second-best all-around player in the league—behind teammate Jordan.

When the season ended, the Bulls had an incredible 67-15 record, a full 10 games better than any other team in the league. Jordan led the league in scoring for a sixth straight year with a 30.1 average. Scottie was the fourteenth best scorer with a 21.0 average. He was also the team's second-best rebounder behind Horace Grant with a 7.7 per game average. In addition, he led the team in assists with a 7.0 mark. He joined Jordan on the NBA's All-Defensive team and was second team all-NBA.

In the playoffs the Bulls whipped the Miami Heat in three straight, then defeated the Knicks in seven tough games before winning the conference crown in six over Cleveland. In the finals they took the Portland Trail Blazers in six games for their second straight NBA title.

In the six-game championship series, Jordan averaged 35.8 points a game. Scottie had a 20.8 average while leading the team with 50 rebounds and 46 assists. He was playing incredible all-around basketball.

It was Bill Walton, the former All-Star center-turned-broadcaster who said what many people were thinking: "You think about it. Scottie Pippen might just be the second-best all-around player in the league. Who's better, outside of Michael?"

From 1990 to 1993, the Bulls were a smooth-running basketball team. Pippen's emergence as a genuine superstar to complement the great Michael Jordan really made the team a force in the NBA. *(John Biever photo)*

In a way the focus on Jordan might have been good for Scottie. Jerry Krause agreed: "I think coming here made it easier for Scottie. If he had gone to another team—a kid from Arkansas, from an NAIA school picked fifth in the draft—the pressure would have been unbelievable. He would have been asked to produce right away. Here there was no pressure. Michael took all the pressure, and Scottie had time to grow. Plus there was a lot he learned from Michael."

After the 1992 season Scottie was a member of the Olympic Dream Team. He joined all the other greats—Jordan, Magic, Bird, Barkley, Ewing, Mullin, Malone, Robinson, and Drexler—on perhaps the greatest team ever assembled. Scottie was running in fast company.

Then it was back to action. The Bulls were out to "three-peat"—win a third successive NBA title. During the regular season the Bulls won their division with a 57-25 record. But the Knicks with 60 wins and Phoenix Suns with 62 had better records, and it was thought that either of those teams had a good chance of unseating Chicago.

Jordan tied Wilt Chamberlain's record by winning his seventh consecutive scoring title. Scottie averaged 18.6, led the team in minutes played, was first in assists and second in rebounds. Once again he was voted to the NBA's All-Defensive team. And he did it playing on a bad ankle for the better part of the season.

The playoffs took a strange turn. After Chicago swept both Atlanta and Cleveland, they then came up against the tough Knicks for the conference title. The Knicks won the first two games at Madison Square Garden, but after that the Bulls stormed back. They won the third, then rode a 54-point Jordan performance to tie the series in game four. But aside from that, Jordan wasn't shooting well. And Scottie picked up much of the slack in the series.

The Bulls won the fifth, and in the sixth Scottie really took over. In the fourth quarter with the Knicks rallying, he hit two clutch jumpers to keep the Bulls in front. When it ended, he had 24 points, 7 assists, and 6 rebounds. And back in game five he'd had two key blocks of Charles Smith layup tries that would have won it in the closing seconds. His work had helped put the Bulls in the finals.

"It's no secret," said Phil Jackson. "So goes Scottie Pippen, so goes Chicago."

That wasn't to undervalue Jordan's contributions, but everyone knew that Jordan was usually nothing less than great. When Pippen also played great, the team became almost unbeatable.

Someone also commented on how well Scottie could run both the fast-break and half court offenses. "Nobody knows how hard I worked alone on dribbling and just feeling the ball in my hands," Scottie said.

From there, the Bulls went on to defeat the Phoenix Suns in six games to take their third straight title. Jordan was the MVP with a brilliant six games in which he averaged 41.0 points per contest. But Scottie checked in at 21.2, and once again led the Bulls in assists and was second to Grant in rebounds.

Then came the terrible off-season in which Michael Jordan's father was tragically murdered in a roadside robbery. Shortly thereafter Jordan shocked the sports world by announcing his retirement from basketball. That meant the 1993–94 Bulls would be without their longtime superstar. Many felt the team would crash. Scottie and his teammates thought otherwise.

With Pippen leading the way, the Bulls surprised a lot of people. The team finished with a 55-27 record, two games behind Atlanta in the Central. Despite an early-season injury that caused him to miss 10 games, Scottie wound up leading the team with a career best 22.0 average. He was the eighth-best scorer in the league.

He was also second in steals and in the top twenty in assists, the only non-full-time point guard in the group. He would never be the scorer Jordan was. No one ever has been. But he was certainly a superstar in his own right.

In the playoffs it came down to the Bulls and Knicks again, this time in the Eastern Conference semifinals. Playing at home, the Knicks won the first two. The Bulls knew they had to adjust.

"I don't think our problem is offense," said Scottie. "I think it's stopping them on defense and not letting them get second shots. We have to win the third game."

The third game in Chicago was unusual and exciting. The Bulls actually blew a 22-point lead and, trailing by one, needed a last-second basket to win it. Coach Jackson set up a shot for Toni Kukoc, the rookie from Europe. And when the Bulls returned to the court, Scottie was on the bench. The play worked perfectly, and Kukoc hit the long three-point jumper to give the Bulls a 104–102 victory.

Later it came out that Scottie had just sat out on his own. Maybe it was pride or competitiveness, but he wanted that shot. Suddenly there was controversy. Before game four Scottie made a statement. "I put it behind me," he said. "I apologized to the team and to Phil Jackson. I don't think I have to apologize to anyone else."

Guard B. J. Armstrong spoke to the rest of the Bulls when he said, "I don't care what he did. He's my teammate and I'm going to back him up. This team is the twelve players. We just need to support him right now."

Scottie thanked his teammates by going out and scoring 25 points, grabbing 8 rebounds, and garnering 6 assists as the Bulls won the fourth game, 95–83, to tie the series. Then came the controversial fifth game. The Bulls had a one-point lead with just 2.1 seconds left when Hubert Davis tried a long jumper. Scottie got up in his face, and Davis missed the shot. But the ref whistled a controversial foul and Davis made both free throws to give the Knicks an 87–86 win. It was a turning point.

Chicago won the sixth game 93–79. Had there not been a foul call at the end of game five, the series would have been over. With the seventh game at Madison Square Garden, the Knicks' defense finally ended the Bulls three-year reign. New York won it, 87–77, despite a 20-point, 16-rebound effort from Scottie.

But the Bulls had gone down like true champions, fighting to the end. Sure, they missed Jordan. What team wouldn't? Yet, without him, they were still one of the best teams in the league. Much of the credit for that had to go to Scottie Pippen and the way he had led the team all year.

There was a time when Scottie had said, "I honestly don't know whether I could function as a player away from Michael now." But when he had to play without Jordan, he proved again just how good he was. For a small-town, small-college kid from Arkansas, that's quite an accomplishment.

As Scottie himself said on still another occasion. "When I'm healthy, there isn't a challenge in the world I can't meet."

DAVID ROBINSON

HAD DAVID ROBINSON FINISHED GROWING BEFORE HE entered the Naval Academy, he might now be well on his way to a brilliant career as a navy officer. Sure, he would have been a 6'7" officer, but that was all right with the navy. The normal height limit to enter the academy is 6'6". But there was an exception to the rule. It stated that 5 percent of the incoming class could be as tall as 6'8".

The navy's loss, however, was basketball's gain. After entering the academy, David continued to grow—and grow and grow. When he graduated in 1987 he was a full 7'1" and coming off a season as college basketball's Player of the Year. In addition, he wasn't projected as simply a journeyman NBA center. People were talking about him as a future superstar.

But a basketball future had to wait. First David had a naval obligation to fulfill, which he did without question or qualm. He was drafted by the NBA's San Antonio Spurs. The team knew it would have to wait several years before he could join them. The question was—would the wait be worth it?

David Maurice Robinson was born on August 6, 1965, in Key West, Florida. Ambrose and Freda Robinson had two other children, Kim and Chuck. All three children grew up in Virginia Beach, Virginia, where Ambrose Robinson was a sonar technician in the U.S. Navy. A career navy man, Mr. Robinson was often away at sea for up to six months at a time.

Freda Robinson worked as a nurse, which meant the children were left on their own often. But they were always given very specific instructions as to what their responsibilities were.

"We always knew the difference between right and wrong," David said. "We had a lot of responsibilities, but we had a lot of freedom, too. For that reason, I never felt any desire to break loose."

David was an intelligent and curious youngster. As early as the first grade he was enrolled in a program for gifted children.

When Mr. Robinson was home, he spent a lot of time with his family. Young David followed his father everywhere, watching how he did things and trying to do them on his own. When he was 12, he finished putting together a television his father had bought as a surprise for his mother.

"My dad was the person I patterned myself after," David has said. "I never had any sports role models as a youngster. My dad was everything to me."

Unlike most other great athletes, David didn't get caught up in sports at a young age. He played ball with his friends, but just for fun. He was more interested in his studies and in learning. David grew slowly and wasn't really tall for his age until he reached high school.

As a freshman, David attended Green Run High School in Virginia Beach. He went out for the basketball team as a freshman, but soon left the squad. Though he had grown to 6'4" as a sophomore, he didn't go out for the team again. Then in the fall of 1982, Ambrose Robinson retired from the navy and took a job near Manassas, Virginia, which was near Washington, D.C.

David was just starting his senior year and would now be going to Osbourn Park High. He was 6'7", tall enough for basketball coaches to notice him. But David's goal was to attend the U.S. Naval Academy. He liked their math and engineering programs, as well as the secure future the navy would offer. So he was working very hard to get an appointment to the academy.

Basketball was an afterthought, but he agreed to go out for the team. When the starting center sprained an ankle, David suddenly got the job.

"I hadn't played a lot of street ball," David admitted, "so I didn't have the moves, those intuitive things that kids learn on the playgrounds over the years. In those early years basketball was more work than fun. I knew I could prove myself academically. But with basketball, it was just a matter of trying to stick it out."

Coach Art Payne said he could see that David would someday be a quality player, but he had a lot to learn. The team finished the year at 12-12 with David as the leading scorer and rebounder.

"We were a hair away from being a real solid team," Coach Payne said. "The difference was David's inexperience. He averaged about 14 points a game, but he was inconsistent and that hurt us."

Then the coach added, "David also wasn't caught up in the enthusiasm of the game yet. I think that started to come toward the end of the season. But he really still didn't know what he could do out there."

More important to David were his grades. When he scored an excellent 1,320 on the SATs, he received an appointment to the U.S. Naval Academy at Annapolis, Maryland. Basketball was still on the back burner for him.

But the coaches at navy saw him as a potential player for them. "We thought he could become a solid running forward," said assistant coach Pete Hermann. "His hands were pretty good and he could run. What he needed was more strength and stamina, but that was something he could develop. What none of us envisioned when we first saw him was that he would eventually become a center."

David entered the academy at 6'7", but by the time he actually arrived at Annapolis he was up to 6'9" and still growing. So he went out for basketball, but not with a great deal of enthusiasm.

In fact, David admitted that there were times his freshman year when he would be sitting in sixth period math class and say to himself, "Oh, brother, I have to go to basketball practice today."

Navy had a good scrappy team that year and finished the season with a 24-8 record, the most wins in the history of the academy. David averaged just thirteen minutes a game, scoring at a 7.6 per game pace. He had 111 rebounds and 37 blocked shots. One positive note was his 62.3 shooting percentage, thirteenth best among returning players in the country.

Academically, David had adjusted well. He had a 3.22 grade point average (out of a possible 4.0), so his studies were well under control. During the summer he lifted weights and played in a summer league. When he returned for his sophomore year he had grown two inches, to 6'11", and put on 20 pounds. He was now 215 pounds and getting stronger.

There was little doubt that he was now a center. The starting center from the year before had graduated, so the job was now David's to win or lose. Coach Evans decided to put some pressure on the youngster and build the offense around him.

Service academy teams aren't usually among the best in the country. For one thing, the height restriction prevents the recruiting of tall players. A guy like David, coming in at 6'7" and then shooting up to 6'11", was unusual. To compensate for their lack of height, the teams are usually well conditioned and fundamentally sound. That's the kind of ball club Navy had in 1984–85.

The coaches kept the offense simple because of David's inexperience, and the concept worked. With players like Vernon Butler, Kylor Whitaker, and Doug Wojcik all contributing, David and his fellow Midshipmen began to win. David scored 29 points in an 84–68 win over American University in the third game of the year. Soon after that, the team went to Southern Illinois University to participate in the Saluki Shootout Tournament.

Though the Middies lost to host Southern Illinois in the semifinals, David was becoming a force. He scored 31 points against the favored Salukis. Then in the consolation game with Western Illinois, he erupted for 37 points and 18 rebounds as Navy won, 80–74.

He was scoring with short turnaround jumps, a variety of drives and dunks. He was becoming fun to watch.

Teammate Doug Wojcik said the tournament marked a turning point in David's career. "From then on, David realized he could be a pretty good player," said Wojcik. "Of course he turned out to be more than pretty good."

Navy finished the season at 26-6, the best record in the history of the academy. The team received a bid to the NCAA tournament and upset Louisiana State before losing to Maryland. David averaged 23.6 points a game for the year, a huge improvement over his first season. He also had 11.6 rebounds a game and blocked 128 shots. Among all the sophomores in the country, David was second in scoring and first in rebounding, blocked shots, and field goal percentage. He was on his way.

Though the eyes of the NBA were already turning toward David, everyone was aware that he would owe the navy five years of active duty after he graduated. That could put any chance for a professional basketball career on hold forever. But David would finish what he started.

All five Middie starters were back for the 1985–86 season. With the team now firmly centered around David, they began to win again. After losing to powerful St. John's in their opener, the Midshipmen won 14 of the next 16. And during this time, David was playing better and better.

In a game against the University of North Carolina–Wilmington on January 4, he was all over the court on defense. When the game ended, he had blocked an amazing fourteen shots. With David leading the way, Navy was suddenly nationally ranked, a lofty position that service academy teams rarely achieve.

More numbers began coming. David scored 37 points in one game, then grabbed a career best 25 rebounds in another. The Middies won their conference tournament, then went to the NCAA championships once again.

Against Tulsa, David scored 30 points and grabbed 12 boards in an 86–68 Navy win. Next came powerful Syracuse. With David scoring 35 points and grabbing 11 rebounds, the Middies won the game, 97–85.

"David is as good a big man as there is in the country," said Syracuse coach Jim Boeheim. "He just killed us."

Finally Navy was in the East Regional final against Duke. One more victory and the ball club would have been headed for the fabled Final Four. But the overall speed of Duke finished Navy. David tried with 23 points and 10 boards, but All-American guard Johnny Dawkins led a running attack that took the Blue Devils to a 71–50 win and eliminated Navy from the tournament.

Navy had ended the year with an impressive 30-5 record, its best ever. And David had averaged 22.7 points and a national best 455 rebounds, a 13.0 average. He also led the entire country with 207 blocked shots. He made several first team All-American squads and was named to the second team in several other polls. There was no denying that he had become one of the very best big men in the country.

After leading the U.S. team to a gold medal in the World Championships in Spain during the summer, David returned to Annapolis for his final year. He was now 7'1" and 235 pounds.

Not only did David grow a full six inches while at Navy, he also emerged as a genuine All-American. Here he towers over the opposition as he blocks yet another shot. *(Courtesy United States Naval Academy)*

Some of the other top players had graduated, and Pete Hermann had been promoted to head coach. David knew he would have to carry a greater load than ever, and it didn't take long to see that he was ready. In the opener against North Carolina State, he exploded for 36 points, though the team lost, 86–84.

Against the smaller schools he was virtually unstoppable. He had 45 against James Madison and 44 versus Drexel. There was little doubt that he was now the best collegiate big man in the country.

At midseason something happened that would change David's future. The navy decided that once David graduated he would be commissioned in the naval reserve, not the regular navy. That meant he would serve only two years of active duty instead of five. Some thought it was a case of an athlete getting preferential treatment. But in reality the navy felt that David was simply too tall for a commission as an unrestricted line officer.

The decision meant that playing pro ball was now more of a reality. But before dealing with that, David still had to finish his career with Navy.

Against powerful Kentucky, he scored 45 points, grabbed 14 rebounds, and blocked 10 shots, even though the Middies were beaten. That game was on national TV, and David was a secret no more. He led his team to a 26-5 record in the regular season, helping Navy secure another bid to the NCAA tournament.

The Middies had a tough draw. In their first East Regional game they were paired against the Michigan Wolverines. David scored a career high 50 points, but it wasn't good enough. Michigan won, 97–82, ending Navy's season as well as the collegiate career of David Robinson.

He finished the season with 903 points for a 28.2 average, third best among Division I players. He also averaged 11.4 rebounds, fourth best, and blocked a nation's best 144 shots. His reward was to be named a consensus All-American and college basketball's Player of the Year.

In June of 1987 David graduated from the Naval Academy with a degree in mathematics. In early July Ensign David Robinson reported to the navy submarine base at Kings Bay, Georgia, to begin serving his two years. If an NBA team drafted him, it would also have to wait two years for him.

The team that had the first pick in the 1987 draft was the San Antonio Spurs. They made their decision quickly and without hesitation: David Robinson—even if they had to wait two years.

David began negotiating with the Spurs. That November it was announced that he had signed a $26 million pact spread over eight years. Though he wouldn't be playing for two years, he was already one of the best paid players in team sports. The Spurs obviously thought of him as a player worth waiting for.

David played some international ball during his two-year navy hitch, including the Pan American Games as well as the 1988 Olympics. He looked rusty both times, leading people to question his value to the Spurs. David was discharged from the navy on May 19, 1989, and then began working toward the basketball season. He knew it wouldn't be easy.

"For me, the biggest thing is to come out and get some confidence so I can play the way I know I'm capable of playing," he said. "I have to bring my whole game around, keep learning. There is always something to learn.

"I haven't felt this way in a long time. This is a new challenge, and I love challenges."

David looked good in the preseason. He showed he was as fast or faster than any big man in the league. His timing was back, and that made his rebounding and shot blocking even more effective. Some felt he would quickly take his place beside the two premiere centers in the league, Patrick Ewing of the Knicks and Hakeem Olajuwon of the Houston Rockets.

The Spurs opened their season against Magic Johnson and the Los Angeles Lakers before 15,868 fans at the HemisFair Arena in San Antonio. The Lakers came out with the intention of intimidating the lanky rookie. But it only took one quarter of NBA action to show that wouldn't work.

In the second quarter David began asserting himself. A spectacular block of a Magic Johnson shot off a drive got everyone pumped up, and the Spurs went on to win, 106–98. It was a great debut and a portent of things to come. Even Magic Johnson was impressed.

"Some rookies are never really rookies," said the Magic man. "Robinson is one of them."

Both David and the Spurs got off quickly. It was apparent that this was a different San Antonio team, one that would not be easy to beat. By the end of December the ball club had a 19-7 record and was in first place in the Midwest Division. (After 26 games a year earlier, the Spurs had been just the opposite, 7-19.) A month later the team was still winning at 29-13 with a league-best 19-1 record at home.

As for David, his numbers were up with the other top centers, and he was already being talked about in the same breath as Ewing and Olajuwon. Veteran center Caldwell Jones, brought in to help David develop, said he was already there. "He has the talent all us big guys only hope and dream for," Jones said. "No other big guy I've ever seen is as quick and fast as David. That's what really sets him apart."

"He has everything," Golden State coach Don Nelson said of David, "strength, quickness, size, and speed."

David continued to play consistent basketball for the rest of the year. When it ended, the Spurs had a 56-26 mark, winning the Midwest Division and finishing with the fourth best record in the entire league. They also finished 35 games better than the season before, making it the biggest turnaround from one season to the next in NBA history.

As for David, he finished with 1,993 points in 82 games. That was good for a 24.3 average, tenth best in the league. David's 983 rebounds (a 12.0 average) placed him second behind Olajuwon, and he was third in blocked shots with 3.89 per game. Thus it came as no surprise when he was named NBA Rookie of the Year.

In the playoffs, the Spurs began by eliminating the Denver Nuggets in three games led by David and point guard Rod Stickland. Next came the powerful Portland Trail Blazers. The two clubs battled for seven full games, with the Blazers finally coming out on top, 108–105, in the deciding contest.

David remained consistent. In 10 playoff games he averaged 24.3 points, 12 rebounds, and 4 blocks. And despite the loss, he wound up on the third All-NBA team and second All-Defensive team. In one year, after two years away from the game, he had become an NBA force.

He was even better the next year, becoming a first team All-Star and a member of the All-Defensive team. He led the league in rebounding, was second in blocked shots and averaged 25.6 points a game. The team finished at 55-27, winning the Midwest Division once again. This time, however, they were upset in the first round by Golden State.

For the next two years David's reputation as one of the best solidified, but the team couldn't get over the next plateau in the playoffs. There were also some coaching changes and player movement. A torn ligament in his left hand ended David's 1991–92 season after 68 games. But he still led the league in blocked shots with 4.49 per game and was an NBA first teamer again. He was also on the All-Defensive team and, better yet, was named Defensive Player of the Year.

In 1992–93 he was an All-Star Game starter for the third straight year and once again put up solid numbers. The club finished at 49-33 that year, but after beating Portland in four games in the first round of the playoffs, they lost to Phoenix in the second round, 4–2. Some began to say that David lacked the fire and determination to bring San Antonio a championship.

Prior to the 1993–94 season David had knee surgery to repair a small tear and remove a cyst that he said had bothered him for the past two seasons. He also looked forward to the Spurs moving into their new home, the AlamoDome, a state-of-the-art stadium that could seat some 65,000 for football and more than 21,000 for basketball.

The team also made a major move, acquiring small forward Dennis Rodman from the Detroit Pistons in return for Sean Elliott. At 6'8" Rodman had defied the odds to become the best rebounder in the NBA. In 1991–92 he grabbed 1,530 boards, an average of 18.7 a game, most in the NBA in twenty years. The next year he did it again. Despite missing 20 games, he averaged

18.3 caroms a game. A tenacious defender who helped the Pistons win a pair of NBA titles, Rodman was expected to bring new life and a winning attitude to a team sometimes considered lackluster.

In fact, some of David's critics had hung that tag on him. They said he played too soft, that he relied too much on finesse and jump shots and didn't balance it with power moves underneath. One writer spoke of a "subtle but undeniable decline in his status around the league."

But it was apparent from the outset of the new season that the Spurs were a different kind of team. The fiery Rodman was again the top rebounder in the league. Not only did that take some of the rebounding pressure off David, but Rodman's aggressive style of play also rubbed off. Suddenly David was playing with a newfound aggressiveness.

Though Rodman and Robinson appeared to be an odd couple who were completely different off the court, they forged a fast friendship that translated into victories. David was quick to praise his new teammate and credit him for his inspired play.

"I've been around Michael Jordan and Charles Barkley and Larry Bird," said David, "but I've learned more about winning from Dennis Rodman than from any player I've ever come in contact with."

Though the team still lacked a true point guard and a real deep bench, they continued to win. At one point they had a 13-game unbeaten streak and won 25 of 30 games to raise their record to 40-16. At the same time David Robinson was putting together the best season of his career. He had a 50-point game against Minnesota and a 46-point effort against Boston.

In addition he produced a rare quadruple double

(34 points, 10 rebounds, 10 assists, and 10 blocks), as well as three triple doubles. Again he credited Rodman for much of his success. "Dennis brings a different kind of fire to the game, a fire you can't help but feel," David said. "I was too much of a gentleman; he was too wild. But he's made the game fun again for me. The best way I can describe it is that I don't feel like I'm going into battle unarmed anymore."

Coming into the final game of the season the Spurs were 54-27 and would finish second to Houston in their division. David was in a neck-and-neck battle with Shaquille O'Neal for the scoring title. Playing the L.A. Clippers, David was hot from the outset, and his teammates kept getting the ball to him. Suddenly he was unstoppable, hitting on hooks, jumpers, and drives.

When the game ended, the Spurs had a 121–97 victory and David Robinson had an unbelievable total of 71 points. Not only had he become just the fourth player in NBA history to score more than 70 points (Wilt Chamberlain, Elgin Baylor, and David Thompson were the others), but he had also edged out O'Neal for his first NBA scoring title.

"It was unbelievable," David said. "My team has been behind me the whole year. They always push me to do a lot of individual things. As a leader, I just try to win games, but tonight they really wanted me to shoot it. When the game started, they were looking for me almost every time down the court."

David finished the year with 2,383 points in 80 games for a 29.8 average, best of his career. O'Neal had 2,377 points in 81 games for a 29.3 mark. That's how close it was. Rodman grabbed 1,367 rebounds for a 17.3 average, giving the team that added dimension.

As a pro, David has improved his jump shot. In 1993–94, he led the entire NBA in scoring, including a 71-point effort in the final game of the season. *(John Biever photo)*

David averaged 10.7 boards a game and was third in blocks with 3.31 per contest.

In the playoffs, the Spurs drew a tough first-round opponent. The Utah Jazz had finished just two games behind San Antonio in the regular season and the teams were very evenly matched. One exception was at guard, where the Jazz duo of John Stockton and Jeff Hornacek were thought to have a big advantage over anyone the Spurs had to offer.

The guard play turned out to be a big difference. The Spurs won the first game at home, 106–89, with David netting 25 points. But the Jazz then upset the Spurs in game two at the AlamoDome, 96–84. Game three at the Delta Center in Utah saw Rodman suspended for his part in a second game fight. The Jazz won easily, whipping the Spurs in a 105–72 embarrassment.

Utah won a close one, 95–90, to win the series in four games. San Antonio was eliminated once again.

Though the team still hasn't come close to that elusive title, the 1993–94 season served to reestablish David Robinson as one of the premiere centers in the NBA. He is still a highly visible spokesman for the NBA and for a number of commercial ventures. His articulate intelligence makes him a sought-after guest on many TV and radio talk shows.

Now settled into a comfortable lifestyle with his wife, Valerie, and son, David Junior, the man known as the Admiral still pursues his varied interests, including the David Robinson Foundation, a Christian charitable organization that supports programs which address the physical and spiritual needs of family. But that should come as no surprise. Years earlier David had said there was more to life than basketball. Now he has found a way to excel at both.

LARRY JOHNSON

THE 1990s PROTOTYPE NBA PLAYER IS A GREAT ATH-
LETE between 6'5" and 6'9" who can do everything on
the court—handle the ball, rebound, run, pass, and
shoot. In other words, a player who is capable of dominating a game.

One young player who embodies these special qualities is Larry Johnson, the 6'7" power forward of the
Charlotte Hornets. At the University of Nevada at
Las Vegas (UNLV) he helped his team to a national
championship and was college basketball's Player of
the Year. Larry became the NBA's number-one draft
choice of the Charlotte Hornets in 1991.

He didn't disappoint. A great first season saw him
named Rookie of the Year. The only thing that slowed
him was a back injury in 1993–94, his third year in the
league. But the respect for Larry is tremendous.

When asked about the player who gave him his
toughest challenge, Chicago's All-Star forward Horace
Grant didn't hesitate. "A healthy Larry Johnson,"

Grant said. "L.J. is strong, quick, and can hit from the outside. People don't realize it, but he's a great defensive player, too. He's got the whole package."

But for Larry Johnson to acquire the so-called whole package, he had to overcome something very dangerous—the mean streets of South Dallas. His perseverance and single-minded dedication are a tribute to his toughness and his character.

Larry was born on March 14, 1969, in Tyler, Texas. As a young boy, he often rode his bicycle through Tyler and past an old trailer where Earl Campbell, a superstar running back at the University of Texas and then for the Houston Oilers, grew up. And right next to the old trailer was the mansion Campbell had built for his mother when he became a pro star. That was something else Larry saw.

Larry's mother, Dortha, was raising her son as a single parent, and had to work hard to give him a good life. In quiet rural Tyler, life wasn't so bad. Young Larry had a lot of friends and began playing sports very early. He grew rapidly and was usually bigger and stronger than the other boys his age.

He began quarterbacking a Pop Warner League football team when he was just nine. Most of the other players were 14. He also took up boxing with the Police Athletic League. He would box for some five years, part of the toughening process he would need when he and his mother moved to South Dallas.

When Larry was twelve, he had to learn to cope with South Dallas, one of the toughest urban ghetto areas in the country. He began hanging out with kids who stole. The police caught him once. There were no charges, but his mother let him sit at the police station until late at night, just to teach him a lesson.

"South Dallas is one of the most messed-up areas I've ever seen," Larry has said. "You had your crack dealers, your cocaine dealers, your dopeheads, and police raids every night."

Larry began playing basketball as often as he could, but life was difficult and dangerous. He played at Green Bay Park and often thought about being hit by a stray bullet. The games themselves were very rough.

"You would have a fight a week," Larry recalls. "If you played Monday through Saturday and didn't have a fight, you knew you had to be ready for one on Sunday."

When he was in the seventh grade he was already 6'2" and weighed 190 pounds. There weren't too many kids willing to mess with him, at least not on an equal basis. That worried some of his friends.

"We didn't worry that Larry would get in trouble," said boyhood friend Alex Gillum. "We worried that other people would be so afraid to fight him with their fists that they would get a gun and shoot him."

Larry continued to play basketball and was the best player in the projects. And even the bad kids acquired an unusual respect for him.

"Those guys were bad," Larry recalls. "I knew it. But they always wanted me to do good. They would tell me when something was going down. They made sure I was out of there."

Next came high school. Larry was already an outstanding player. The area school was Lincoln High, an all-black school with many of the same problems found on the streets. One of Larry's junior high coaches thought Larry would be better off at Skyline High, a racially mixed school some distance away. Larry's mother agreed, and that's where he went, though it was a long bus ride.

Skyline High was different from anything Larry had known. "They called it the Skyline Fashion Show," Larry remembered. "There were all these kids with all kinds of clothes. It was like a miniature college, but I didn't know anyone—at least not until basketball started."

As soon as practice began, ninth grader Larry told the coach, J. D. Mayo, that he felt he was good enough to play with the varsity. But ninth graders, as a rule, didn't play varsity. So when the first game rolled around, Larry started for the freshman team and played well.

"Just before the varsity games started, I suddenly had an idea," J. D. Mayo said. "I thought, Why don't I start the kid just to see how good he really is."

All Larry did was hit all eight shots he took in the first half, adding one free throw for 17 points. At halftime he asked the coach how he was doing.

Coach Mayo had all he could do to contain himself. "If you keep your great attitude and keep working hard," he said, "you'll be fine."

In truth, Larry was already a dominant player who could control a game. That was proved by the fact that Skyline didn't lose a home game in the four years Larry played. He was simply a sensational player who practiced every chance he had. Even after games, he'd go right over to the local recreation center and play some more. Basketball was in his blood.

After Larry's junior year, Coach Mayo told his mother that Larry had a chance to be an NBA star someday. "He knew what he wanted, and he had the body to get it" was the way the coach put it.

As a senior, Larry was 6'5" and over 200 pounds. He was not only the best schoolboy player in Texas, but also one of the very best in the country.

There was little doubt that all the major colleges would be interested in Larry. What few people knew, however, was that Larry was a poor reader. That slowed him down and caused him problems when he took the Scholastic Aptitude Test. The first time he took the test his score was below 700, which meant he wouldn't be eligible to play basketball as a freshman at a four-year college. Because Larry had wanted to attend Southern Methodist University in Dallas, he took the test a second time. This time his score was above 700. The university asked him to take the test a third time, just to be sure.

Larry had to decide what to do. He knew he had to improve his reading skills, which might be tough to do with the pressure of big-time basketball. But he didn't want to sit out a year. That was when he decided to attend Odessa Junior College in Odessa, Texas. He could play ball without pressure and concentrate on his reading.

Larry graduated from Skyline High in June of 1987 and that fall enrolled at Odessa. The 6'7", 230-pound freshman became a hero there as soon as basketball season began. He was incredible. As a freshman he averaged 22 points and 18.1 rebounds. After the season he was named the nation's top freshman by both *Sporting News* and *Basketball Times*. He was also tabbed Junior College Player of the Year.

The next year he checked in at nearly 250 pounds, yet was as quick and agile as ever. He began to put together an amazing string of games. In one he had

51 points. In another he nailed 41, including five shots from three-point range.

Odessa had a 33-2 record that year, as well as a regional title. As for Larry, he averaged 28.3 points and 17.3 rebounds a game. Once again he was named Junior College Player of the Year. Better yet, his reading level was now where it was supposed to be. His decision had been a good one.

"I loved junior college," he said. "I look at my classes at Odessa and know I couldn't have kept up my grades coming [into a four-year college] right out of high school. I tell other guys in my shoes not to go to a four-year school. Do it the way I did."

But now the four-year schools wanted him. Larry began to scout around. He had met a couple of players from the University of Nevada at Las Vegas, Greg Anthony and Stacey Augmon, at the 1988 Olympic trials. They helped convince him that he could help bring the Runnin' Rebels a national championship. So in the fall of 1989, Larry found himself at UNLV.

The team Larry joined at Las Vegas was already strong. The Runnin' Rebels had finished with a 29-8 record the year before and had all their starters returning. Larry would move in at power forward.

He became the team's scoring and rebounding leader right from the outset of the season. Yet he played an unselfish game that made him the team's spiritual leader as well.

"I've never seen anyone like Larry," said teammate Augmon. "And I've never played with anyone as good. There are a lot of gifted athletes on this team, but Larry is the cream of the crop."

Led by Larry and the others, UNLV put together a great season. They lost just four times in the regular schedule and were a top ten team all year long as well as the number one seed in the West Region of the NCAA Tournament.

UNLV swept the region. In the Regional Finals they whipped run-and-gun Loyola Marymount, 131–101. Augmon had 33 points, Anderson Hunt 30, and Anthony 20. Larry also scored 20 and cleaned the boards for 18 rebounds. The team looked like a powerhouse as it headed for the Final Four.

In the semifinals, UNLV came back from a halftime deficit to top a good Georgia Tech team at 90–81. Now they were in the finals, meeting Duke for the national championship. UNLV had never won a national title, and the Rebels came out like a team on a mission.

Larry and company hit 10 of their first 14 shots to jump in front 21–11. They never looked back. From there they marched to a 47–35 halftime lead and, after intermission, kept extending it. They won the game, 103–73, the greatest margin of victory in NCAA history. Hunt was the leading scorer with 29 points, while Larry had 22.

"This is the greatest," Larry said. "But no single player deserves more credit. It has been a real team effort all year."

In forty games Larry had scored 822 points for a 20.6 average. He also averaged 11.4 rebounds a game and had a sensational 62.4 shooting percentage from two-point range. In his first year of major college basketball, Larry Johnson became a consensus All-American.

In 1990–91 the Runnin' Rebels looked stronger than ever. It was hard to see any college team challenging them, so when the regular season ended, UNLV was

Everywhere he has played, Larry Johnson has made an impact and become
a superstar. At the University of Nevada–Las Vegas, he led the team to a
national championship with strong inside play on both offense and defense.
(Courtesy University of Nevada–Las Vegas)

a perfect 27-0. They then won their conference tournament with ease, bringing their mark to 30-0. They were odds-on favorites to win another national title.

In the opening tourney game they whipped Montana, 99–65, and the rout seemed to be on. But the Rebels second-round game with Georgetown produced a bit of a surprise. UNLV won, but the 62–54 margin was surprisingly close. It was only the second time all year that the Rebels had won by less than 10 points.

Then came the West Regional final. This time the Rebels defeated Seton Hall by a 77–65 count. Only once again the team seemed to be lacking something. Larry had a big 30-point game against the Pirates and was named the Outstanding Player in the Regionals. In addition, the team had now won 45 straight games, the fourth-longest winning streak in NCAA annals.

The closeness of the last two games, however, had the coach wondering. "Our intensity has been incredible for most of the year," Jerry Tarkanian said, "but right now it's not incredible."

But the Rebels were returning to the Final Four as expected. In the semifinal game, UNLV would be playing Duke, a rematch of their championship game of a year earlier. The Blue Devils were a very solid team, led by 6'11" Christian Laettner with support from the likes of Bobby Hurley, Grant Hill, Brian Davis, and Thomas Hill. They played extremely well together.

One of the Blue Devils' strategies was obvious from the start. They constantly fronted Larry on defense so his teammates would have a difficult time getting him the ball. On offense, the versatile Laettner would stay outside, drawing Larry away from the defensive boards. The strategy helped give Duke an early 15–6 lead.

Toward the end of the first half, Anthony and Hunt

began hitting from the outside and UNLV managed a 43–41 lead at intermission. But the game was still dangerously close and would stay close for the entire second half. Then with 3:51 left and the Rebels leading 74–71, Anthony took the ball inside on a drive and was called for a charge. It was his fifth foul—he was out.

With their point guard on the bench, the Rebels began struggling. Though a Hunt layup made it 76–71, Duke began rallying. Both Hurley and Thomas Hill connected on clutch three-pointers while the Rebel offense stalled. Suddenly the game was deadlocked at 77–77 with less than a minute to go.

With 12 seconds left, Laettner was fouled. He made both free throws to give the Blue Devils a 79–77 lead. UNLV worked it down for a last shot. It went in to Larry, but he was double-teamed and had to pass it back out to Hunt. Hunt's long jumper glanced off the rim just before the buzzer sounded. Duke had won.

Larry had just 13 points in his final game, the Duke defense having limited him to only 10 shots. His 13 rebounds led both teams, and he was also the leading rebounder in the tournament for the second straight year. He wound up the season with a 22.7 scoring average and grabbed 10.9 rebounds a game.

Once again he was a consensus All-American. But that wasn't all. He was the winner of both the James Naismith award and the John Wooden award, given to the college basketball Player of the Year. In the eyes of nearly everyone, that man was Larry Johnson.

There was little doubt that Dortha Johnson's son had really made something of himself. He did well in his studies at Las Vegas and came close to getting his degree. He vowed to complete it at a later date. And on the basketball court he was surely a winner. In his four years at Odessa and then UNLV, his teams had a combined record of 134–13.

It was now obvious that Larry would be a high pick in the upcoming 1991 NBA draft. Some thought he would even go in the number one spot. But he had his critics, too. There were some who said Larry wasn't really 6'7", was closer to 6'6" or even 6'5". They felt he would be overmatched as an NBA power forward. What those people didn't know was the dimension of his talent, his great strength, and his heart for the game.

The first pick in the 1991 draft belonged to the Charlotte Hornets, a team that had been born to expansion in 1988. The Hornets had won just 20 games their first year and found improvement slow in coming. They needed superstar talent.

The Hornets' coach, Allan Bristow, said that of everyone he had seen, Larry impressed him most. "Larry Johnson doesn't have a weakness," the coach said. "I've been around a lot of great players in my life and all of them had weaknesses. I can't think of a single weakness for Larry."

After that ringing endorsement it came as no surprise that the Hornets made Larry the number one pick in the entire draft. But then Larry's agent and the Hornets couldn't agree on a contract. Larry held out during the preseason, and soon there were rumors that he might to go Europe to play. "I'm ready to play," he said. "I was ready three or four months ago. Nothing has been as terrible as waiting to get into camp."

With the start of the season just a few days away, the two sides finally came to an agreement. Larry signed a six-year contract worth an estimated $20 million. He would receive $1.9 million the first year with the figure going up each year of the contract. Larry was glad to have the negotiations part behind him.

"I don't feel like I'm in game shape," he confessed, "but the only way to do that is to get out there with the team. I feel I can play against the Celtics Friday night. I don't want to miss the first game. My dream has always been to play in the NBA."

Playing just half a game in the opener, Larry scored 14 points. Then the team came home to face the New Jersey Nets. Playing before a crowd of more than 23,000 fans, who gave him a standing ovation, Larry scored 16 points and grabbed 18 rebounds. Who said he couldn't play power forward in the NBA?

He continued to improve his game as the season wore on. The Hornets had a few top-notch players such as 5'3" point guard Muggsy Bogues and sharp-shooters Kendall Gill and Del Curry, but they needed depth and another star to go with Larry.

Like some other exceptional young players who find sudden wealth as pros, Larry was quick to give back. He made substantial donations to Skyline High and Odessa Junior College. He didn't do the same with UNLV because he disagreed with the way the university was treating his former coach, Jerry Tarkanian. Instead, he bought all new equipment for the training rooms at the school. He also gave the Charlotte chapter of the United Way a check for $180,000.

In addition, he bought a home for his mother in Dallas and one for himself in Charlotte. "I love the city of Charlotte," he said. "Everyone has been very friendly and the fans have been great."

He soon was featured in a sneaker commercial in which he donned a wig, glasses, and a frumpy dress.

Despite playing against taller men in the NBA, Larry remains an inside force. His great strength and quickness make him tough to stop on offense and an outstanding rebounder on defense. *(Courtesy Charlotte Hornets)*

He became "Grandmama," the slam-dunking granny who would chew up pretenders on the court.

As the season progressed, Larry matched his skills and strength against the best the NBA had to offer and more than held his own. Though the Hornets finished with a 31-51 record and out of the playoffs, Larry had put together a banner year. He led all rookies with 1,576 points for a 19.2 average. He also grabbed 899 rebounds and that translates to 11.0 a game. Not surprisingly, he was named NBA Rookie of the Year.

"It feels real good to be the first former UNLV player to win the award," Larry said. "The trophy won't be staying in Charlotte. It's going back to Dallas with me, and I'm giving it to my mom."

Then came the 1992 draft, and the Hornets got the second pick this time. They chose a center—6'10" Alonzo Mourning of Georgetown. Mourning wasn't a huge center, but he was a ferocious competitor with great all-around skills.

Once Mourning joined Larry in the Hornets' lineup, the team became winners. The duo formed a young one-two punch perhaps unmatched around the NBA.

At season's end, the Hornets had their best record ever at 44-38. They were in the playoffs for the first time.

Larry led the team in scoring with a 22.1 average, and in rebounding with 10.5 per game. He also led the league in minutes played, as he appeared in all 82 games for the second straight season. He scored a career-best 36 points against Golden State on December 2, and after the season was named to the All-NBA Second Team.

In the playoffs the Hornets upset the Boston Celtics, 3–1, in a best-of-five series before losing to the New

Larry Johnson. *(Courtesy Charlotte Hornets)*

York Knicks in five games of a best-of-seven. The team seemed headed for greater things in 1993–94, but that was before injuries took their toll.

First, Larry learned in the off-season that he had a herniated disk in his back. He didn't need surgery, but the therapy was slow and he was not expected to be at full strength when the 1993–94 season began. But that didn't stop the Hornets from rewriting Larry's contract, and the new one was a headline-grabbing blockbuster.

The new pact, added on to his first contract, covered 12 years and was worth the unheard of sum of $84 million, the largest total contract in the history of sports. Larry, of course, was overjoyed.

But the pact didn't make the 1993–94 season any happier. Money can't buy good health. Larry started the season slowly and was just rounding into shape when he suffered a lower back sprain, unrelated to the disk problem. But this injury caused him to miss 31 games, nearly half the season. In addition, center Mourning sat out 21 games with a leg injury. Without their two stars, the team faltered.

Though both came back near the end and the team finished strong, their 41-41 record wasn't good enough for the playoffs. With a healthy Johnson and Mourning, the Hornets would have been in contention.

Larry played just 51 games, averaging 16.4 points and 8.8 rebounds. His numbers reflected how the back injuries had slowed him down. With luck, Larry Johnson will return and stay healthy. Then the sky should be the limit.

From the streets of South Dallas to the NBA, Larry Johnson has always been a special person and a great player. As Horace Grant put it, Larry Johnson "has got the whole package." And that says it all.

ALONZO MOURNING

THE MID-1990S WAS A TIME FOR THE CHANGING OF THE guard in the National Basketball Association. Fresh names and faces were being touted around the league. Shaq, L.J., Anfernee, Kenny, Chris, Jamal, and Zo are just a few of the players creating new-generation excitement.

Perhaps the most unexpected of these young super-stars is the man they call Zo. Zo is Alonzo Mourning, the aggressive, often combative center of the Charlotte Hornets. Because he played out of position for two years at Georgetown University, his pro potential was a guessing game for even the experts. He was far from the can't-miss pro prospect.

Yet Alonzo Mourning came into the NBA deter-mined to prove himself. He brought with him a work ethic similar to that of his illustrious predecessor at Georgetown, Patrick Ewing. His will to win and to excel was apparent the first time he pulled on a Hor-nets uniform. If Ewing, Hakeem Olajuwon, and David

The man they call "Zo." *(Courtesy Charlotte Hornets)*

Robinson were *the* centers of the mid to late 1980s and early 1990s, then Mourning, Shaquille O'Neal, and Dikembe Mutombo could well be *the* big men taking the game into the twenty-first century.

Alonzo Mourning's trip to the NBA began in Chesapeake, Virginia, where he was born on February 8, 1970. In his early years he began playing sports with his friends without giving much thought to ever playing professionally. Everything was just for fun.

But when young Alonzo was just 12 years old, his entire world changed. His parents split up and left him to live with a friend of theirs, a woman named Fanny Threet. She was one of those rare individuals who, in spite of having a family of her own, found it hard to turn away any youngster who badly needed a home. Over the years she acted as a foster parent to some fifty children.

Fanny Threet gave all her youngsters positive values, including a love of education. Alonzo was always an intelligent youngster who did well in school—if he put his mind to it. Of course, there were times when he didn't do that. Good lessons and habits don't always come easily.

At about the same time his parents split and he went to live with Fanny Threet, Alonzo was exhibiting a real interest in basketball. Besides playing the game with his friends, he often watched college and professional games on television.

He was camped in front of the TV on a March night in 1982 to watch the NCAA championship game between the University of North Carolina and Georgetown University. Carolina had marquee players in James Worthy, Sam Perkins, and freshman Michael Jordan, while

Georgetown nad an exciting seven-foot freshman center named Patrick Ewing.

That was the game in which Ewing, playing on pure adrenaline, swatted away the first four Carolina shots. Each was called goaltending, meaning Ewing had caught the ball on the way down and the baskets counted. But Alonzo Mourning was so impressed with Ewing's shot-blocking exhibition that he never forgot it. And never forgot about Georgetown University.

A short time later Alonzo was playing center in an AAU-sponsored game. That night he did his best imitation of Ewing and every other great center who had ever played the game. Mourning blocked an incredible 27 shots.

By the time he reached Indian River High School in Chesapeake, he was growing rapidly, moving toward his final height of 6'10". In his senior year, 1987–88, he was so good that he was ranked the number one player in the country by Bob Gibbons, who specialized in ranking high school players.

While a number of colleges were ready to go after the services of the 6'10", 240-pound pivotman, Alonzo remembered the Ewing years at Georgetown, which had started with that memorable 1982 championship game. Alonzo liked the Hoyas' aggressive style of play, a pressing, in-your-face defense and a fast-breaking offense. Like Ewing, he was a shot-blocking demon.

In the fall of 1988, Alonzo made the short trip from Chesapeake, Virginia, to Washington, D.C., to begin his studies and basketball career at Georgetown. He felt he was more than ready for John Thompson and his top-notch program.

Coach Thompson had come to the school in 1972

and turned the Hoyas into a national basketball power. The coach was 6'10" and commanded incredible respect from his players. He had been an all-American at Providence College and later played on two Boston Celtics championship teams, backing up the legendary Bill Russell at center.

As a coach, Thompson wanted his teams to play aggressively with an all-for-one and one-for-all mentality. That was Thompson's style as a coach and his formula for success. But as a person, he cared deeply about his players and their education. He knew that college was not just an opportunity to play basketball. He not only sent players to the NBA with regularity but also had a graduation rate of more than 95 percent.

Patrick Ewing, perhaps the best-known player to come out of Georgetown, had received his degree in fine arts right on schedule and graduated with his class. That's why Alonzo's foster mother, Fanny Threet, was overjoyed when he decided to attend Georgetown.

That didn't mean that Alonzo Mourning's years at Georgetown would be easy. He did win the starting center job his first year, just as Patrick Ewing had. So the comparisons started. Alonzo was two inches shorter than Ewing, but had that same dogged determination when going after rebounds and blocks. He also showed a varied offense, being able to take short jump shots and hooks with either hand.

But the Georgetown offense wasn't geared for one player to be a super scorer. Every player, even one with All-American potential, had to fit within the team concept. Alonzo had no problem fitting in with the program. The Hoyas had an outstanding team in

1988–90, featuring high-scoring Charles Smith and Mark Tillmon. As always, the team was deep and Coach Thompson liked shuttling fresh players into the game to keep his frenetic, pressing pace.

In just the third game of the season, Alonzo attracted national attention. Playing against Saint Leo, the Hoyas won easily, 95–62, as the freshman center blocked an amazing 11 shots.

By the end of the regular season the Hoyas were Big East champs with a 23-4 overall record. Then they defeated Boston College, Pittsburgh, and Syracuse to take the Big East Tournament. The team was now ranked number two in the country in both the Association Press and United Press International polls.

With the Hoyas as the number one seed in the East Region of the NCAA tournament, it looked as if Alonzo would duplicate Ewing's feat of leading the club to the Final Four as a freshman. But after beating Princeton, Notre Dame, and North Carolina State, the Hoyas had to face Duke in the regional final, the winner going to the Final Four. Then there was a departure from script. Duke won the game, 85–77, ending the Hoyas outstanding season.

For Alonzo, it had still been a brilliant debut. He'd started all 34 games and averaged 13.1 points and 7.3 rebounds. Some felt he should have grabbed more rebounds, but that criticism was offset by the fact that he led the entire nation with 169 blocked shots. He also shot 60.3 percent from the field.

After the season he was named to the Big East All-Rookie team and was second team All Big East. The widespread respect for his talent was further shown when he won the Big East Defensive Player of the Year prize.

"Mourning has already shown himself to be a talented, big game player," wrote one scribe. "He does many of the same things Patrick Ewing did here and has the potential to follow Ewing as a great pro player."

Maybe that was jumping the gun a bit. There was still plenty of college ball left to be played. And in 1989–90 some things would suddenly change. Georgetown had another center who had seen limited action the year before, but was now improving rapidly. His name was Dikembe Mutombo. Mutombo was born in Africa and hadn't started playing basketball until a few years earlier, but he was 7'2" and beginning to show some real skills, especially on defense. Some were calling him a bigger version of Alonzo Mourning.

That posed a dilemma for Coach Thompson. What if he wanted to play both big men at the same time? The answer was obvious: Mourning, as the slightly smaller and quicker player would have to move to power forward when Mutombo was in the game at center. So, in effect, Alonzo would have to learn a different position.

Despite Alonzo's change to forward and the working of Mutombo into the lineup, the Hoyas won their first 14 games. But after that, they struggled a bit. There were regular season losses to Connecticut, Syracuse (twice), Providence, and Seton Hall.

After that the team lost in the second round of the Big East tournament and then in the second round of the NCAA Midwest Regionals, this time to Xavier of Ohio, 74–71. It had still been a 24-7 season, but it was a disappointment.

Alonzo had started all 31 games and had his scoring average up to 16.5 per game. But Mutombo grabbed

325 rebounds to lead the team with 10.5 per game. Zo had 265 for an 8.5 average. The big change was in blocked shots. After leading the nation with 169 his freshman year, Mourning had just 69 as a sophomore. Mutombo was getting more of the blocking chances because he was playing the middle. Despite the change, Zo was still Co-Defensive Player of the Year in the Big East and a first team All-Big East selection.

He was a sociology major now, and his grades had improved since his freshman year when he hadn't always taken the academic work at Georgetown seriously. Coach Thompson had helped his young star put things in perspective. Thompson made him realize that he had to explore all the possibilities within himself, not just the athletic ones.

"I cut down on the parties after that," Zo admitted. "That was part of keeping things in perspective. There will always be parties. Now I have other priorities."

That didn't make his junior year any easier. Mutombo was established at center now, and Zo knew he'd be spending most of his time at power forward. Some tried to tell him that playing forward would help him, make him a better passer, and enable him to see the court better, but that didn't help when the Hoyas went into a full court press and only Mutombo sat back to clog the middle while Zo sat out part of the time on the bench.

He also suffered the first serious injury of his career, a strained arch in his left foot. The injury came during the fourth game of the season, a game in which Zo was outplaying Duke's All-American forward, Christian Laettner. Georgetown would win the game, 79–74. Before Zo was injured, he had scored 22 points and pulled down 10 rebounds. Laettner had just 14 points on 5-for-22 shooting.

Georgetown was 4-0 at the time of Alonzo's injury. While he sat out, the team was 6-3. When he returned, his play was inconsistent. He had some good scoring games, but also some games when he seemed to disappear. It was apparent that he just wasn't comfortable at power forward.

At the same time, the Georgetown season disappeared. The team didn't have the depth of the previous two years; it also lacked scoring punch. The Hoyas wound up losing five of their last regular season games, then were beaten by Syracuse in the final of the Big East tournament. They still got an NCAA bid, but lost in the second round of the West Regionals, 62–54, to eventual national champ UNLV.

Alonzo wound up with a 15.8 average in 23 games. He also grabbed 7.7 rebounds and blocked just 55 shots. Mutombo led the club with a 12.2 rebounding average and scored at a 15.2 clip. After the season, he would become the number one draft choice of the Denver Nuggets.

There was also a question of Alonzo coming out early, going to the NBA. He ended the speculation in his own way. "My foster mother has never seen me play once," he said. "But nothing will stop her from coming to my graduation."

Coach Thompson went a bit further. "When I asked him last spring what he was going to do, stay or leave, he said he thought he needed to mature some more. I told him I thought he was correct. End of story."

Alonzo also had something to prove. Since his sensational freshman year, his stock had dropped. There were no honors after his junior year, and some were wondering just what kind of pro player he would make. Coach Thompson said there was a good reason for what had happened. It had nothing to do with Alonzo's skills. "Dikembe was the new kid on the block, and the new kid on the block is always the big deal," Thompson said. "Last year Zo would have gotten all the blocked shots and rebounds Dikembe got if I had put Zo at center."

Well, he would be back at center in 1991–92. Instead of playing organized ball during the summer, he worked out at Georgetown with his friends, Ewing and Mutombo. He also worked for Congressman Thomas Bliley of Virginia. So it was a relatively quiet summer, free from the strain of competition. But when he returned to Georgetown he was ready. "I feel like a volcano ready to erupt," he said.

That was bad news for the Hoyas' opponents. The club opened the season playing in a tournament in Hawaii. They beat Hawaii-Loa, 101–76 and Hawaii-Pacific, 95–65. In those two games Alonzo had 56 points, 24 rebounds, and 14 blocked shots. Two games later against Delaware State he had 22 rebounds and 9 blocks. And several games later, when the Hoyas opened their Big East schedule against Villanova, Zo checked in with 24 points, 15 rebounds, and 8 blocks.

It was apparent to everyone that Alonzo was once again a dominant player, a force in the middle, a shot-blocking demon who was now back at center full-time and prospering. People even noticed a difference in his attitude. "Alonzo had gotten away from that chippiness he once had," said Boston College Coach Jim O'Brien.

It was true. Zo had made a conscious effort to control his competitive instincts and to avoid becoming too combative and even hostile.

"You can't take the emotion out of a player," he said, "and emotion has been with me since I played my first organized game in seventh grade. But I've tried to control it. I look at things with more of an eye to how they'll affect me in the long run. Is it going to stain my image or disrupt me mentally or physically.

"My freshman year I definitely didn't think that way. Now I say to myself, 'Hey, that's not the road to go. Despite all the negative things that have happened, I've been able to come out on top.'"

Unfortunately the Hoyas still didn't have a great all-around team to support Alonzo. But he continued to play very hard every night, and his stock once again rose with the NBA scouts and general managers canvassing the colleges.

Some of the spotlight was deflected away from him, however, by another center who was attracting national attention. Shaquille O'Neal was a 7'1", 300-pound junior at Louisiana State who was already being touted as the next great center in the NBA. It was also assumed that if he decided to forgo his senior year and turn pro, he'd be the NBA's number-one pick.

One coach who thought Mourning was at or near the top of the pro prospect list was Jim O'Brien. The Boston College mentor put it this way: "If O'Neal doesn't come out, I can't believe [Alonzo's] not number one, [Christian] Laettner included. And I think Laettner's a great player." Laettner, of course, was Duke's 6'11" All-American forward, a player of multiple capabilities. But now Zo was ranked right up there with him.

Mourning continued to put together a string of great games. Against Villanova he had 24 points, 15 rebounds, and 8 blocks. He scored 28, added 12 rebounds and 4 blocks in a win over Providence. He had 26 points and 7 blocks against Miami and a big 38 points with 16 rebounds and 6 blocks in a two-point loss to Boston College.

He was doing this despite being the most fouled player in the country. The Big East was experimenting with six personal fouls before disqualification instead of the usual collegiate five. So the games were rough and Zo kept going to the line, where he buried more than 75 percent of his free throws.

Boston College center Bill Curley, who had a number of major battles with Alonzo, described what it was like to go up against the Georgetown star: "He gets up so quickly that he could probably catch some of those shots he blocks. It's as if someone's throwing him a lob. He can just tap the ball out to a teammate, like an outlet pass."

Others had noticed that subtle change in Zo's game. Many shot blockers prefer to slam the rejected shot as hard as they can, even pounding it into the crowd. That might look spectacular, but it also returns the ball to the offensive team. Zo was very adept at tapping the rejection to a teammate, thereby putting his team on offense.

When the season ended, the Hoyas had a 22-10 mark. They lost in the Big East tournament finals to Syracuse once again and were eliminated from the NCAA tournament in the second round by Florida State. But Alonzo had had a great senior year, averaging 21.3 points and 10.7 rebounds a game. He also blocked 160 shots, an average of 5.0 a game. He hit on 59.5 percent of his shots from field and 75.8 percent from the line.

After the season he was named an Associated Press first team All-American. He also made a number of other All-American squads. He was Big East Defensive Player of the Year and Eastern Basketball Player of the Year. In addition, he was also a finalist for both the Wooden and Naismith awards, the two major Player of the Year selections. Both prizes went to Laettner, but Alonzo was the winner of the Henry Iba Defensive Player of the Year award.

Alonzo left Georgetown as the school's fourth highest career scorer and third best rebounder. His 453 blocks were second only to Ewing's in total and his 3.77 per game was a school best. Had he played center all four years his numbers would have been even better.

He also left Georgetown with something else—a bachelor's degree in sociology. Like Ewing before him, Zo graduated with his class. Now he awaited the NBA draft to see where he would be playing as a pro.

The Orlando Magic had the first pick in the 1992 draft, and to no one's surprise they took Shaquille O'Neal. The Shaq had announced he was coming out early, and the Magic grabbed him. The second selection belonged to the Charlotte Hornets. The Hornets were an expansion team that had started play in 1988. Like most expansion clubs, the Hornets struggled for the first few years. Then, in 1991, things began looking up.

That was when the Hornets drafted Larry Johnson, the great forward from UNLV and College Player of the Year, on the first round. Johnson stepped in and averaged 19.2 points and 11.0 rebounds to become the

NBA's Rookie of the Year. But the Hornets still finished at 31-51 and out of the playoffs.

With a chance to get a second franchise-type player, the Hornets decided to pass on Christian Laettner and take Alonzo Mourning as the second pick behind O'Neal. They hoped that would give the club a one-two punch that would propel them into the playoffs.

After sitting out the preseason in a contract dispute, Zo finally signed a multiyear, multimillion-dollar deal and joined his new teammates. It didn't take long to see that he fit the NBA like a glove. Maybe he wasn't as tall as the Ewings, the Olajuwons, the Robinsons, and the O'Neals, but he was just as talented, tough, and determined. He wanted to show that he could play with anyone.

Part of the reason Alonzo was able to work his way into the lineup without much fanfare was the public's fascination with Shaquille O'Neal. Among the fans and the media, it was Shaq this and Shaq that. The big guy began making commercials, singing with rap groups, and playing great basketball. He was a larger-than-life superstar and the next dominant center.

But in his own way Alonzo Mourning was nearly as effective. His numbers weren't quite up to Shaq's, but some were already saying that he had the better all-around skills. One of his boosters was another long-time superstar, Charles Barkley. "Alonzo Mourning is going to be the next great, great, unbelievable player," Barkley said. "Shaquille, in my opinion, is a great physical specimen."

Zo meshed immediately with Larry Johnson, and the whole team put together a winning season, finishing at 44-38 and making the playoffs for the first time in their history.

At 6'10", Alonzo isn't as tall as some of the other top NBA centers. But his talent, toughness, and tenacity have enabled him to do battle with anyone and become a real superstar. *(Courtesy Charlotte Hornets)*

As for Zo, he more than lived up to his advance billing. In 78 games he scored 1,639 points for an average of 21.0 a game. He also grabbed 805 rebounds, an average of 10.3 a contest. In addition, he had 271 blocked shots. That was fourth best in the league behind Olajuwon, O'Neal, and his old teammate Mutombo. He had more blocks than David Robinson and Ewing.

By contrast, rookie O'Neal averaged 23.4 points and 13.9 rebounds. So he did edge Zo in the major statistical categories and would be named Rookie of the Year.

In the playoffs, Charlotte shocked the Boston Celtics by eliminating them in four games, 3–1. But then they came up against the defensive-minded New York Knicks and couldn't get it done. New York won in five games, 4–1.

But Zo had elevated his game in the playoffs, especially against former Georgetown star Ewing. In nine playoff games, Zo averaged 23.8 points and 10.0 rebounds, leading the Hornets in both departments. There was little doubt that he had arrived.

During the off-season, Zo continued to work on his game, often squaring off against Ewing and Mutombo back at Georgetown. All three former Hoya centers remained close, good friends. And they were still in constant touch with Coach Thompson. Yet when they squared off against one another, it was war.

"The bottom line is about wanting to be the best," Zo said. "I'm motivated by any player who tries to keep me from doing what I want."

Some tried to create a rivalry between the two young centers, Shaq and Zo. They said the two might bring back the classic rivalry between Wilt Chamberlain and Bill Russell in the 1950s and 1960s. Pat Williams, the general manager of the Orlando Magic (Shaq's team), was one who played it up. "I think people see a reincarnation of Chamberlain and Russell," he said. "Power, size, and brute strength against Mourning's quickness, agility, and hostility. The far bigger player, the true Goliath, being combated by the smaller, more agile, maybe more athletic center."

Alonzo would have none of this. To him, playing the NBA games meant doing the same thing against everybody, not just Shaq. He wouldn't play along. "I'm not hyping up some rivalry," he told reporters. "That's your little game, trying to create this rivalry. I'm not into that. You guys cooked this whole thing up, but I don't get excited by it at all."

Alonzo was more into winning. He had never had the taste of a national championship at Georgetown, so his goal now was simple: an NBA championship.

The Hornets tried to fine-tune the team prior to 1993–94. They traded Kendall Gill and picked up shooting guard Hersey Hawkins and veteran forward Eddie Johnson. The team was hoping to move up another notch, close to the league's elite. But problems started right from the beginning. Larry Johnson had a herniated disk that he worked to rehabilitate prior to the season, but when play began, he was at less than full strength.

Alonzo had to shoulder more of the load at the outset. Then, just as Johnson seemed to be gaining strength, he suffered another back injury, a lower back strain. He would end up missing 31 games and not playing like the old Larry Johnson until the final weeks of the season.

Zo was great in December. He had 18 rebounds in

a game against the Celtics and also had two straight games when he scored 36 points. For the month he averaged 23.9 points and 10.2 rebounds. Then, between December 30 and January 11, he missed six games with a sprained ankle. He returned with a vengeance, getting 11 offensive rebounds against the Lakers on January 14. He had eight blocks in a January 25 game against Miami.

In late January he was chosen as a reserve on the Eastern Conference All-Star team. But on January 28 he tore a muscle in his left calf and would be out until March 8. He missed 16 games, including the All-Star Game. In the 22 games Zo missed (including a one-game suspension) the Hornets were 6-16.

With both players back, the club rallied in the final weeks to finish the year at 41-41. But they missed the playoffs by a single game. In 60 games, Zo averaged 21.5 points with a high game of 39 in the home finale against Detroit. He had 610 rebounds, 10.2 a game. His 188 blocked shots for an average of 3.13 per game placed him fourth in the league behind Mutombo, Olajuwon, and Robinson. There is little doubt about the quality of his play now.

Alonzo Mourning is one of the bright new stars of the NBA. Like Patrick Ewing and Dikembe Mutombo, he prospered under John Thompson at Georgetown and matured as soon as he entered the NBA. With his desire and competitiveness, Zo will be more than ready to challenge Shaquille O'Neal as the NBA's premier pivotman as the NBA moves toward the twenty-first century.

Shaquille O'Neal

The Shaq came to the NBA in 1992, and there isn't a basketball fan anywhere who doesn't know what the Shaq Attaq is. The Shaq is Shaquille O'Neal, the 7'1", 300-pound center of the Orlando Magic, who is already one of the most recognizable athletes in the world, not to mention one of the best centers in the NBA.

Shaquille joined the Magic after three outstanding seasons at Louisiana State University, and his arrival on the pro scene was one of those right-place-at-the-right-time situations. As it turned out, Shaquille's first year would be Michael Jordan's last, and the NBA didn't have to look far for its next highly visible and marketable marquee player.

The Shaq was a natural showman, a precocious twenty-year-old who quickly showed he could handle the pressure of being in the limelight as well as the wear and tear of an 82-game NBA season. He was outstanding at both. Shaquille also became a prime figure in the NBA's practice of marketing its individual stars amid a team concept. And he helped to put the expansion Magic on the map.

Shaquille O'Neal was born on March 6, 1972, in Newark, New Jersey, a tough city that had been torn apart by street riots back in 1967. It wasn't an easy place to live. People in the inner city had to contend with poor living conditions, crime, and drugs.

Shaquille's father, Philip Harrison, decided he didn't want his family staying in Newark, so Mr. Harrison joined the army. But before he could marry Lucille O'Neal and find another place to live, he was sent overseas. Shaquille was born while his father was away and before his parents could marry.

Lucille O'Neal paged through a book of Islamic names and finally picked Shaquille Rashaun for her newborn son. The name means "Little Warrior" in Arabic. She didn't know it at the time, but her son would grow up to be anything but little. "I wanted my children to have unique names," Lucille O'Neal said. "Having a name that means something makes you special."

Sergeant Philip Harrison returned a short time later. The first thing he did was marry Lucille O'Neal, but Shaquille would keep his mother's maiden name. Philip Harrison had decided to make the army his career. That would mean moving his family around from base to base, including two stays in Germany.

Moving wasn't easy for a fast-growing youngster, Shaquille remembers. "Meeting people, getting tight with them, and then having to leave was the worst part," he said. "Sometimes when you came into a new place they tested you. I was teased a lot—teased about my name, teased about my size, teased that I should be in a higher grade in school because I was so big."

Before long, however, there was something good in Shaquille's life. That something was basketball. When Shaquille was 13 years old his family was sent back to Germany. He was in junior high school and was already 6'6" tall.

Dale Brown, the basketball coach at Louisiana State University, came to the army base to run a basketball clinic. When he saw Shaquille, Coach Brown thought he was a soldier and asked him his rank.

"I don't have a rank, sir," Shaquille answered. "I'm just thirteen years old."

Brown couldn't believe it. He also wouldn't forget it. Here was a 6'6" kid who could play basketball, and he was just 13. Brown made sure that he and his coaching staff kept in touch with the family and followed the career of young Shaquille.

The stay in Germany wasn't easy for Shaquille, but Sergeant Harrison gave his son a piece of advice that would stay with him. He said the world had too many followers and not enough leaders. Shaquille would have to choose which he wanted to be. "I told him there was no half-steppin' in his life," Sergeant Harrison said.

Shaquille made his decision: he would try to be a leader. By the time the family returned to the United States, Shaquille was ready for high school. He would be attending Robert G. Cole High in San Antonio, Texas. The school was located on the army base at Fort Sam Houston. And the kid who was ready to enter his junior year was now 6'8" and 240 pounds.

It was at Cole High that Shaquille's basketball career really started. He was just 15 years old in the fall of 1987, but he wasn't a clumsy and awkward kid. His father had taught him the fundamentals of the game, and Shaquille could already run the floor and move quickly; he had great agility for a youngster his size. The team was built around him from his very first game.

With Shaquille in the middle, Cole went unbeaten during the regular season, only to lose to Liberty Hills in the state playoffs. This was largely because the big guy had four fouls in the first quarter and was pulled by Coach Dave Madura for much of the game. Yet not many teams finish 32-1. The coach quickly decided his goal for the next year was to be state champion.

The coach also asked one of his former players, Herb More, to come back to Cole as an assistant coach. More, who was 6'6" tall, would work with Shaquille, who by now was 6'10" and 250 pounds. This was something More looked forward to.

That summer Shaquille played in a local league, where he dominated all the other big men. Then he played in two tournaments, one in Phoenix and another in Houston. The result was the same: Shaquille was the best big man on the court.

"I think that's really when people began to see that he was going to be special," Herb More said.

Even before basketball season started in 1988 the colleges began their recruiting efforts. Dale Brown of LSU had stayed in touch with Shaquille after meeting him in Germany. Once the other schools learned that Louisiana State wanted Shaquille, they began coming around as well.

Shaquille's father and Coach Madura handled most of the recruiters. They were interested in coaches who talked about education first. Shaquille visited a few schools, but by November he had made up his mind. Before his high school senior year started, he had decided to attend Louisiana State.

"The final decision was his alone," said his father. "It was time for him to apply the things we'd taught him and the things he had learned in life, and do what he had to do."

But before he could go to college, Shaquille had to finish up at Cole. He had a brilliant final season. He'd been taught to play an all-around game, and despite his size, Shaquille became a complete player.

It was a dominating year for him. Despite being double- and triple-teamed, he averaged more than 30 points and 20 rebounds in a 32-minute high school game. And he did it despite having to sit out for long periods.

Cole was unbeaten in the regular season and then began the playoffs. In one game Shaquille had a career high of 47 points. In another he burst across the lane after a missed Cole shot, caught the rebound low in his left hand, and in one motion brought the ball up and slammed it through the hoop. The rival coach said that play was "NBA material or nothing is."

In the title game against Clarksville, Shaquille had 19 points and 26 rebounds to lead his team to a 66–60 victory and the state championship. Cole was 36-0 for the year with Shaquille O'Neal averaging 32.1 points and 22 rebounds a game. He was a *Parade* All-American selection and by the end of the year stood an even seven feet tall and weighed 275 pounds!

Shaquille graduated from Cole High in June of 1989. Now he was ready for the next phase of his life—a big-time collegiate program at LSU.

The main thing on his mind was his education when

Shaquille entered Louisiana State University at Baton Rouge in the fall of 1989. He knew that one serious injury could alter or end his basketball career, so he always made sure to pay attention to his studies, and he kept his grades up the entire time he was at LSU. But there was little doubt that basketball would consume a great deal of his time.

The LSU Tigers of 1989–90 already had a pair of potential stars. Sophomore guard Chris Jackson was a fine ball handler and shooter, a potential All-American. Stanley Roberts was a 7'0", 260-pound center who hadn't played his first year at LSU but was ready now. Shaquille checked in at 7'1" and 295 pounds. Coach Brown and his assistant, Craig Carse, would have to juggle the two big men.

"Stanley was much more skilled offensively then," Coach Carse said, "but Shaquille had that tremendous work ethic. He was a great athlete who could run the court like a guard, had the tenacity to pull down rims, and played a hard, intimidating game. Stanley played more of a finesse game."

For the first few games Roberts started at center with Shaquille coming off the bench. Jackson was off to a spectacular start, scoring 37, 32, and 27 points in the first three games. Roberts led all rebounders with 13, 12, and 15. But in game four Shaquille began to assert himself, grabbing 17 big rebounds in a Tiger victory over Lamar. After that, Shaquille became a starter and the highlights began coming.

The Tigers finished the year with a 23-9 record as O'Neal averaged 13.9 points and 12 rebounds a contest. He also set a Southeastern Conference record with 115 blocked shots. He fouled out of nine games and had to sit out parts of others because of foul trouble, so there was plenty of room for improvement, but his potential was so great it scared people.

When he returned for his sophomore year he was a bona fide 300-pounder, all muscle. Assistant coach Craig Carse observed that "he doesn't have any fat on him." Shaquille also improved his vertical leap by an amazing eight inches. He could now touch a spot nearly two and a half feet above the rim.

But there was also a big change in the team. Chris Jackson left to enter the NBA draft, and Stanley Roberts had decided to play professionally in Spain. So the 1990–91 Tigers would be built around Shaquille and two other youngsters, Maurice Williamson and Vernel Singleton.

It was also about this time that Shaquille began referring to himself by a new nickname—Shaq, and that's what it has remained.

His thunderous dunks would bring crowds to their feet, and soon the expression "Shaq Attaq" was coined. More highlights began coming. Playing against the tall front line of Arizona, Shaq took on future NBA stars Sean Rooks, Brian Williams, and Chris Mills. All he did was score 29 points and grab 14 rebounds in 28 minutes as LSU won, 92–82.

"I'd heard stuff out there—that I was just another player," Shaq said, "that I was too young. I wanted to show I could play with anybody."

In the very next game, against Arkansas, he scored an amazing 53 points while grabbing 19 boards. There was little doubt now that he was one of the most dominant players in the country, college or pro.

LSU would finish the season at 20-10, losing in the first round of the NCAA tournament, which was a big disappointment. But after it ended, Shaquille began

At Louisiana State University, defenders hung all over Shaq whenever he went into the paint. Still he became an All-American. *(John Biever photo)*

collecting honors. He was a consensus first team All-American selection in addition to being named Southeastern Conference Player of the Year. Then the Associated Press, United Press International, and *Sports Illustrated* all named him College Player of the Year.

Playing in twenty-eight games, he averaged 27.6 points and 14.7 rebounds, leading the nation in the latter category. He also blocked 140 shots, a national record for a sophomore.

There was some talk that Shaq wanted to leave LSU and turn pro, but his father said that money wasn't a good enough reason to leave. So the big guy returned for his junior year and the 1991–92 basketball season. But something had changed. It was the way the other teams were trying to stop the mountain in the middle.

"Shaquille just wasn't able to play his game that year," said Craig Carse. "They were trying everything possible to stop him. Anything to rile him—kidney shots, talking trash, or just hitting him as he ran downcourt."

Shaq didn't complain, but it was obvious the other teams' tactics were taking their toll. The Tigers finished at 21-10, eventually losing to Indiana in the second round of the NCAA tournament 89–79. Shaquille had 36 points and 12 rebounds, but it wasn't enough.

Once again Shaq was a consensus All-American. He was second in the nation in rebounding with a 14.0 average and led the country with 157 blocks. More postseason awards followed. Now there was a serious question—would Shaq return to LSU for his senior year?

He didn't keep people guessing for long. On April 3, a news conference was called at the Baton Rouge campus of LSU. Shaq announced that he would forgo his senior year to enter the NBA draft. And he said his well-thought-out decision was based on a lot more than money. The rough and sometimes dirty tactics used against him had taken their toll.

"I was taught at a young age that if you're not having fun at something, then it's time to go. When I told my father, he realized it wasn't the money, but because I wasn't having any fun. He finally said, 'If I was you, I'd want to leave, too.'"

As soon as Shaq made his announcement, all the teams that were in the draft lottery and had a shot at the first pick began revising their plans. A chance to get a franchise center doesn't come along often.

When the draw was held to see which team would have the first pick, the Orlando Magic got the nod. They were an expansion team in 1989–90 and would start their fourth season in 1992. When they had a chance to pick Shaquille, they didn't hesitate for even a split second. They finally reached agreement with Shaq on a seven-year pact worth an amazing $39.9 million, the biggest contract given to a rookie player in any sport.

Shaquille was obviously pleased, but he didn't want people to think he could make the Magic champions all by himself. "I'm not rushing into anything," he said. "If I'm not a dominant player my first year, I'll still be okay in the long run."

Some felt he was just being modest. After watching Shaq play in a summer league, Magic Johnson offered this prediction: "Shaq will be great, and I mean *great!* The guy is a monster, a true prime-time player."

Even before he played his first NBA game, Shaq was in demand for a multitude of endorsements. He had a kind of boyish charm that came across well on television. He also related well to young audiences, partly because of his love of rap music. Before long he would be one of the most visible athletes in the world.

Shaq didn't mind the early pressure, though. "I don't believe in pressure," he said, "I'm too young to worry. I just relax. I know there are a lot of expectations. If I become a great center like Chamberlain or Russell or Kareem or Walton, that's good. If not, I'll live a happy life and keep a smile."

Shaquille's pro debut came on November 6, 1992, when the Magic played host to the Miami Heat. He played a low-key, conservative game and concentrated on his defense and rebounding. When it ended, Orlando had a 110–100 victory as Shaq finished with 12 points and 18 big rebounds. He also blocked three shots.

It wasn't long before he began to assert himself on both ends of the court. He scored 35 points in a losing effort against Charlotte, then had 31 points and 21 rebounds as the Magic defeated Washington. Then he had 29 points in three straight games. The Magic got off to a surprising 5-2 start, and Shaq became the first rookie ever to be named NBA Player of the Week his first week in the league.

Golden State coach Don Nelson summed up Shaq's game this way. "I had no idea he'd score so much," Nelson said. "Some day he's going to be the best center in the league. He's got all the tools."

Shaq continued to play well. By the end of November the Magic were a surprising 8-3. Houston's great All-Star center, Hakeem Olajuwon, gave the rookie the supreme compliment when he said, "You know what he looks like? A bigger me."

The Magic, of course, were still a young team with

weaknesses. One player cannot make a mediocre team a big winner. Shaq made a difference, but the bench wasn't deep and the team was sometimes inconsistent. At midseason they were a game over .500 at 21-20, and Shaq was voted the starting center on the Eastern Conference All-Star team. At that time he was eighth in the league in scoring, averaging 23.7 points a game. His 14.3 rebounding average was second and his 3.97 blocks third best in the league.

Shortly before the All-Star Game, Shaq showed his power when he pulled down the rim and backboard in a game at Phoenix after one of his thunderous dunks. "I've hit them a lot harder than that," Shaq said. I was a little surprised, but when it started coming down, I started running the other way."

The O'Neal legend was growing. Veteran Mike Sanders of Cleveland said that Shaquille "attacks the basket like no one I've ever seen. I want to see the guy who would think of attempting to block one of his dunks. I guarantee that he'd break your hand if you tried it."

Shaq kept a healthy attitude all year, never letting the praise go to his head. "My main job is to block shots and rebound," he said at one point. "But I think fans get a kick out of seeing me dive on the floor for a loose ball or crash into the seats trying to keep the ball inbounds."

The Magic battled for their first playoff berth. The struggle came down to the final game. Orlando beat Atlanta in that one, 104–85, to finish the season at 41-41, a .500 record. Their best yet. But Indiana also finished at 41-41, and they were given the eighth and final playoff berth, because they had won the season series over Orlando.

Not making the playoffs was a disappointment, but Shaq and the Magic had had an outstanding year. The big guy had played in 81 games, scoring 1,893 points for an average of 23.4, eighth best in the league. He'd had 1,122 rebounds, a 13.8 average, coming in second to Detroit's Dennis Rodman. His 286 blocks, a 3.5 average, put him second, behind Hakeem Olajuwon. He was also fourth in field goal percentage (56.2). Not surprisingly, he was named NBA Rookie of the Year by an overwhelming margin.

"I'm very happy and very proud to win this," said Shaq. "It's been a long year, but I learned a lot and I'm already looking forward to next season."

Because they didn't make the playoffs, the Magic were again in the draft lottery. Though the odds were against their getting the top pick, luck was with them. This time the Magic chose Chris Webber, a 6'9" forward from Michigan and a player who was considered a potential superstar.

But the team felt it needed something more. Within 20 minutes, Orlando traded the rights to Webber to the Golden State Warriors. In return they received the number-three pick in the draft. He was Anfernee Hardaway of Memphis State, a 6'7" point guard considered one of the most exciting all-around college players.

The trade worked well for both teams. Webber would become Rookie of the Year, with Hardaway finishing a close second. Sure enough, the exciting Hardaway was a do-it-all player who formed a great one-two punch with Shaq. In 1993–94 the Magic stepped up another notch to become one of the better—if not yet elite—teams in the NBA.

Despite a busy off-season in which he shot myriad

commercials, cut a rap CD, and played a featured role in the motion picture *Blue Chips,* Shaq was ready to go when the 1993–94 season started. Hardaway proved early he was the real goods, plus the bench was deeper than the year before.

The Magic surprised a lot of people by finishing with a 50-32 record, good for second place in the Atlantic Division, behind the New York Knicks. Shaq had another banner season. For most of the year he battled San Antonio's David Robinson for the scoring title.

At one point late in the season, Shaq riddled the Minnesota Timberwolves' defense for 53 points, edging past Robinson once again. Shaq was averaging 29.34 points per game to Robinson's 29.27.

"The way Shaq's playing now he could get a hundred points one night," said New Jersey Nets coach Chuck Daly.

The battle came down to the very last game. In that one, Robinson exploded for 71 points against the Clippers, while Shaq had to settle for 32 in the Magic's final game against the Nets. That enabled Robinson to edge Shaq for the title, 29.79 to 29.35. But Shaq had a fine year. In addition to his scoring, he was second in rebounding with a 13.2 average. He was still getting better.

The Magic then looked forward to their first post-season appearance. In the first round they had to meet the Indiana Pacers in a best-of-five series. The opening game, played at Orlando, looked like an easy win for the Magic. They led most of the way, only to lose in the final seconds as Byron Scott sank a clutch three-pointer. The final was 89–88. Shaq led all scorers with 26, but it wasn't enough.

With the Orlando Magic, Shaq often towers over his opponents. Once he gets the basketball in close, watch out! *(John Biever photo)*

In the second game the Indiana defense circled around Shaq and limited him to a season-low 15 points. The Magic did battle back from seven down in the final quarter to make it a game, but they were still beaten 103–101. Suddenly the team was on the brink of elimination.

Game three followed the same pattern. The Magic led for three quarters before the Pacers exploded for a 31–14 fourth-quarter advantage and a 99–86 win. Orlando had been eliminated in three straight. Most observers felt it wasn't that Shaq and his teammates had played badly; the Pacers had simply played better.

"I have nothing to be ashamed of," Shaq said afterward. "This was a learning experience for me and my teammates. Believe me, we'll all be back."

There wasn't much doubt about that. The big kid with the quick smile had certainly become an NBA force in the middle. He would finish fourth in the NBA balloting and continue with another busy off-season. In addition to all his commercials and endorsements, there was a new one, a series of Shaq Attaq toys, action figures produced by Kenner.

So the making of a legend continues. The marketing people handle the off-court part of it, while Shaq takes care of business on the hardwood. And there's little doubt that he's still got a way to go before reaching his peak. That's bad news for everyone who has to play against him.

About the Author

Bill Gutman has been an avid sports fan ever since he can remember. A freelance writer for twenty-two years, he has done profiles and bios of many of today's sports heroes. Mr. Gutman has written about all of the major sports and some lesser ones as well. In addition to profiles and bios, he has also written sports instructional books and sports fiction. He is the author of Archway's *Sports Illustrated* series; *Shaquille O'Neal: A Biography; Michael Jordan: A Biography;* and *Great Sports Upsets,* available from Archway Paperbacks. Currently, he lives in Dover Plains, New York, with his wife and family.